MISSING PIECES

3

TYNDALE HOUSE PUBLISHERS, INC., CAROL STREAM, ILLINOIS

RED ROCK MYSTERIES

#1 BEST-SELLING AUTHORS

JERRY B. JENKINS · CHRIS FABRY

Visit Tyndale's exciting Web site for kids at www.tyndale.com/kids.

TYNDALE and Tyndale's quill logo are registered trademarks of Tyndale House Publishers, Inc.

The Tyndale Kids logo is a trademark of Tyndale House Publishers, Inc.

Missing Pieces

Designed by Jacqueline L. Nuñez

Edited by Lorie Popp

Published in association with the literary agency of Alive Communications, Inc., 7680 Goddard Street, Suite 200, Colorado Springs, CO 80920.

Scripture quotations are taken from the *Holy Bible,* New Living Translation, copyright © 1996, 2004 by Tyndale House Foundation. Used by permission of Tyndale House Publishers, Inc., Carol Stream, Illinois 60188. All rights reserved.

For manufacturing information regarding this product, please call 1-800-323-9400.

Library of Congress Cataloging-in-Publication Data

Jenkins, Jerry B.
  Missing pieces / Jerry B. Jenkins; Chris Fabry.
    p. cm. — (Red rock mysteries)
  Summary: Red Rock suffers a spate of "mailbox baseball" vandalism and twins Bryce and Ashley become witnesses.
    ISBN 978-1-4143-0142-6 (softcover)
    [1. Vandalism—Fiction. 2. Stepfamilies—Fiction. 3. Twins—Fiction. 4. Family life—Fiction. 5. Christian life—Fiction. 6. Mystery and detective stories.] I. Fabry, Chris, date. II. Title.
  PZ7.J4138Mis 2005
  [Fic]—dc22   2004030078

Printed in the United States of America

17
12   11   10

"Or suppose a woman has **TEN SILVER COINS** and loses one. Won't she **LIGHT A LAMP** and sweep the entire house and **SEARCH CAREFULLY** until she finds it?"

JESUS
Luke 15:8

CHAPTER 1

❋ Ashley ❋

This story is about a dead girl, a dead dog, a dead mom, and lots of dead mailboxes, so if you don't like dead things, stop reading right now.

For as long as I can remember, my mother has bought a new jigsaw puzzle every few months. She says it helps our family work together on at least one thing. The newest was a picture of a waterfall, nice and peaceful, unlike our lives the past few weeks.

When you first start a puzzle, it's hard to imagine getting finished. But piece by piece it comes together, kind of like life. Well, some people's lives. I don't know if our lives will ever fit together. I can't imagine what the picture would look like in the end.

But with all the dead things in this story, I think you'll be surprised how much life came from it.

◔ *Bryce* ◔

As we set up the tent in our backyard late Wednesday afternoon, I couldn't get my mind off Ashley's doctor's appointment the
next day. Ashley was having an EEG the next morning, and I was
supposed to help her stay up. EEG stands for electro-something-or-
other, but whatever it is, it scares her.

Sam grilled burgers and hot dogs on our back deck. (If you're
wondering why I call him Sam instead of Dad, it's a long story. My
real father was killed in a plane crash. Sam is our stepdad. I've called
him Dad like twice, but Sam feels right to me.)

Dylan, our little brother, kept eating watermelon. Later he ran to the bathroom and stayed there most of the evening. He's a funny little kid, and we all like having him around until he gets annoying.

We made a small campfire in a pit toward the back of the yard and roasted marshmallows, made s'mores, and watched the sun go down. Leigh, our older stepsister, showed up with her boyfriend, Randy. She was excited about her driver's test next week. We joked about telling people to stay off the road.

"Leigh's a good driver," Mom said, looking her in the eye. "She'll be fine."

"Does that mean she can drive me to dance practice next week?" Ashley said.

Mom dipped her head and looked over the top of her glasses. "We'll talk about that."

Dylan came outside crying because he couldn't camp out with Ashley and me. I told Mom we'd watch him until he fell asleep and then carry him inside. She tucked him in to his Scooby Doo sleeping bag.

"Don't let the monsters get you," Randy said before he and Leigh went inside.

"Ooh, good one, Randy," I said, a cold wind whipping the tent flap.

A coyote yipped in the distance, and I glanced at the red rocks rising behind us. The air turned nippy as a crow flew overhead and cawed.

I was glad I didn't have to have stuff stuck to my head the next day like Ashley, but being her twin, I felt bad for her.

CHAPTER 3

✖ Ashley ✖

I love the smell of a campfire. I'm an expert marshmallow cooker, so I showed Bryce how to get the marshmallow just right at the end of the stick. He didn't listen, and his first one fell into the fire. Can you spell s-t-u-b-b-o-r-n?

Dylan popped his head out of the tent. While Bryce tried again, I gave Dylan a couple of plain marshmallows and told him to lie down.

I was nervous about my EEG the next day, not because it hurts or anything, but because last time the doctor said we'd have to try "something different." I don't know what that means, but I was hoping I'd get better rather than worse.

An EEG reads the waves in your brain. Mine do weird stuff when I sleep, and if we can't make things better, my brain could remember those weird signals and I could just pass out even during the day.

I kept telling Dylan to lie down, and he giggled and scrunched into his sleeping bag. When I yelled at him, he stuck his head inside his sleeping bag and Bryce frowned.

We had only a few weeks left of school, and I was glad seventh grade was almost over. We started talking about the summer and what we would do. Earning money was at the top of the list.

Bryce said something about a bike trip with his friend Jeff Alexander. "And I'm going to get a paper route and use my ATV," he whispered.

"Good luck," I said. We ride our ATVs to school, but we're not allowed to ride them on the street. "I'm going to talk with Mr. Crumpus and see if I can roll silverware at the Toot Toot Café."

"They don't let kids our age work."

"I can try."

Headlights passed our house, and the driver gunned the engine. Not many people live past us on our road. What was going on out there?

CHAPTER 4

◎ *Bryce* ◎

I could tell it was a truck, and whoever was inside whooped and yelled. Then the tires spun gravel.

"Probably high schoolers joyriding," I said.

I picked up Dylan—sleeping bag and all—and he rolled over and hugged my neck as I carried him inside. I laid him gently on his bed. He opened his eyes and stared at me, like he wanted to say something. But then his eyes shut, and he was out again.

I pulled the sleeping bag up around him and tiptoed out. When I closed the door, I heard the roar of the truck and glanced out a front window. Our house is set back from the road, but I could see the truck clearly. A strange light flashed inside the cab—it glowed. I saw faces, at least two, but I couldn't make out who.

One of the passengers rolled down the window and held something outside. The truck sped up and went behind a tree. I heard a loud explosion, like someone had set off a cherry bomb. The truck sped away with more whooping and shouting.

I raced through the kitchen and into the backyard and met Ashley coming toward the house. Her eyes were wide. "Did they crash?" she said.

I shook my head and told her what I had seen. We rushed to the tent and grabbed our flashlights.

CHAPTER 5

❀ Ashley ❀

We flew around the house with our flashlights focused on the end of the driveway. Bryce didn't seem as scared as I was. I just hoped no one was hurt.

"Maybe we should get Sam," I said.

Bryce rolled his eyes. I hate when he does that. It makes me feel so stupid.

I expected to see twisted metal, a car on fire, or mangled bodies. I've seen a couple of really bad car wrecks, and the memory sticks with you.

We stopped at the end of the driveway and panned our flashlights to the other side of the road, where I noticed a couple of broken bottles. No crashed cars. No bodies. I couldn't imagine what had made the metallic crashing sound.

"Oh no," Bryce said, moaning. "Look."

He pointed his flashlight at our mailbox. Mom had picked out a big one so she could send and receive her manuscripts. She'd painted flowers on the side, rising like vines, and had let Bryce and me help.

Now the mailbox seemed to cling to the post with its last ounce of strength. It lay flat, the flowers bent, and the red flag Bryce had painted with white stripes and stars hung near the ground.

"Why would they do that?" I said, gasping.

"Mailbox baseball," Bryce said. "Guys ride around with a baseball bat and flatten mailboxes as they drive by. It's some kind of a stupid contest." He was silent a minute. Then, "It was like a member of our family. How many orders from eBay and Amazon.com came in that big old thing?"

"Mom's going to be mad. We should call the police."

Bryce already had his cell phone out. Since we've dealt with them so much in the past few months, he had the number memorized. We walked down the road far enough to see that our neighbors' mailboxes were also smashed. Bryce told the police what had happened and which direction the truck was going.

Bryce closed his phone. "They said they've had a bunch of these this spring and thanked me for calling."

"Think they'll catch 'em?"

Bryce shook his head. "If they don't, I'd like to."

CHAPTER 6

◑ *Bryce* ◑

We woke Sam and he followed us outside. He studied the mailbox and cocked his head. "I'd say that was a home run, wouldn't you?"

I couldn't believe he was being so good about it.

Sam told us to camp out in the living room. I guess he thought whoever had done it might round the bases again. I wanted to bury the old mailbox, but he said the police might want to look at it.

Ashley and I played Monopoly while we watched an old movie. I could tell she was nervous about the EEG, because she didn't buy Park Place when she had the chance. Plus, she didn't choose to be the dog. She's always the dog, but tonight she picked the shoe.

By 3 a.m. I was so tired I couldn't keep my eyes open. I went to bed and didn't wake up until after she was gone. I wanted to tell her good luck, even though I don't really believe in luck.

CHAPTER 7

❋ Ashley ❋

I don't pretend to know how prayer works, but I believe it does. Don't get me wrong. God doesn't always answer the way I'd like, but I do believe he hears everything we pray, whether out loud or in our minds.

I used to wonder about all the people in the world praying at the same time. It seemed impossible that God could hear everybody and answer, but I guess that's because I don't know how much God can do. I mean, how could he speak the world into existence? I don't understand it, but I know he can do it.

Still, sometimes I worry about my prayers and what I ask for.

There are people in the world who don't have enough food or medicine for a sick child. So it makes me feel a little silly to pray for my cat Patches' hair ball or my ingrown toenail. But I think God cares what we care about and wants us to talk to him. In Sunday school class I asked people to pray about my EEG.

As Sam and I walked into the doctor's office, I could almost feel people's prayers.

"Ashley?" the nurse said, the one I'd had since we moved to Colorado. She looks like what you'd expect a nurse who gets along with kids to look like. Her perfume has a hint of lilacs and makes me want to sleep for a hundred years.

As she hooked the electrodes to my head she asked how I was doing since she had last seen me. I hardly knew where to begin.

We talked as she worked, and finally the machine was ready. "You know the drill, Ashley," she said. "Just relax and try to sleep. When you wake up, Dr. Alek will see you and your dad."

She turned the lights low. My eyes were tired, and it felt good to drift off. Before I fell asleep, I prayed one last time. *Help my brain do what it's supposed to do and not what it's not supposed to do.*

It was kind of lame, but I knew God would understand.

CHAPTER 8

◎ *Bryce* ◎

Mom let me go back to sleep until third period, then drove me to school. We didn't talk about Ashley's appointment, but I could tell Mom was worried.

I checked in at the office and hurried to my class. The bell had just rung, and people milled around the halls. I caught bits of conversation.

"... whole thing was smashed ..."

"... don't have any idea who did it ..."

"... my dad was so angry ..."

So our part of town wasn't the only one hit by the vandals.

Skeeter Messler asked why I was late. He's kind of got a thing for Ashley, poor guy.

"I was up late with my sister."

"Ashley? Is something wrong?"

"Doctor's appointment this morning. She has to sleep during the tests, so she stays up late."

Skeeter looked away like he had just heard that Colorado had been invaded by killer koalas. "I had no idea."

"She's had this a long time," I said.

"Is she in the hospital?"

"No," I said, slamming my locker. "She'll be back tomorrow."

I could tell Skeeter's mind was running, and I hoped Ashley wouldn't hold me responsible for anything he did. While we walked to our third period class, I changed the subject to damaged mailboxes. Skeeter hadn't seen any.

At lunch I realized I'd forgotten to pack mine and I hadn't brought money. My stomach growled. I scanned the lunchroom, stopping on a terrifying sight. She sat next to a small cash register at the end of the line. I was about to go into uncharted waters, where an undertow could take you out to sea.

I was about to face every kid's nightmare at Red Rock Middle School.

The Lunch Lady.

CHAPTER 9

❀ Ashley ❀

In the waiting room I found Sam talking to the mother and father of a little boy on the floor. The boy smiled at me as he played with LEGOs. He was missing two teeth on top and one on the bottom, so he looked like he had been in a fight.

"This is Ashley," his mother said. "She just finished doing the same thing you're going to do."

"How old are you?" I said.

"Seven."

He seemed small for seven. His mom and dad just stared at him.

"Does it hurt?" the boy said.

I got down on the floor with him and shook my head. "You just go to sleep." I lowered my head so he could see where the nurse had put the electrodes. "The nurse is really nice. She'll put this gunky stuff in your hair, but it washes out in the shower."

The nurse stuck her head out the door. "Ian?"

He stood and glanced at his mother.

"You want me to go with you?" I said.

He smiled again, and it looked like he had an acre of gums. His mouth was a crossword puzzle with too many holes. And four down didn't line up with three across, if you know what I mean. I walked back with him and showed him the chair he would sleep in and the computer. He climbed in the chair while the nurse went to work.

"Thank you," she whispered as I left.

It was near lunchtime when the nurse finally ushered Sam and me into another room. Sam kept checking his watch.

Finally, Dr. Alek came in and apologized for being late. "Who's the big troublemaker here?" he said, looking at me. "Is it you, Ashley? Are you the troublemaker?"

Dr. Alek is from the Middle East, so he talks kind of funny and fast. He has large, black eyebrows and short hair. He's about as tall as Mom, and his nose is pointy. He wears a blue medical coat with a stethoscope hanging out of the front pocket. We hated leaving our old doctor in Illinois, but when we found Dr. Alek, Mom said our prayers had been answered.

"Stand up, Ashley," he said. He pulled my arms to my sides, had me close my eyes and touch my nose with my index finger. He checked my reflexes, tapping my legs and arms with a little rubber hammer, looked in my eyes and ears with a special light, tossed a ball to me and had me catch it, and then asked me to sit down.

Sam was quiet the whole time, just watching.

Dr. Alek made a few notes in my folder, then closed it and faced Sam. "Any problems at night? Any recurrences?"

"Not that we can tell," Sam said. "Something wrong?"

Dr. Alek looked at his chart again and seemed to try to smile. "I wish I could give you better news. The last few EEGs show the discharges in the brain getting worse."

Sam asked questions, but I couldn't concentrate. I felt like my life was over.

"What do we do?" Sam said.

"Try different medication. Unfortunately, this is not an exact science. Different people respond differently to medication. We have to find what works." Dr. Alek looked at me like my head was on backward.

I didn't feel any different. "Am I going to be this way for the rest of my life?" I said.

He leaned close. "I had hoped we'd be further along by now, that you wouldn't need to keep taking pills and having these tests. But no, I still have hope that you will be able to beat this." He tousled my hair. "You're a big troublemaker, you know that?"

I knew he was teasing, but still it almost made me cry. I figured that was because I was so tired.

He wrote a new prescription and showed Sam how to wean me from the medicine I was already taking and start the new stuff.

The nurse at the front smiled. "Ian's mom said to tell you thanks."

"Did he do okay?"

"Slept like a baby." She handed me a Tootsie Pop from a basket filled with buttons and stickers and candy. "Don't worry, kiddo. We're going to get you better, you'll see."

CHAPTER 10

○ *Bryce* ○

Maybe the Lunch Lady's hairnet reminds me of a nightmare, or it could be the way she looks at us or yells at us for the smallest thing. Some kids say she lives in an old house with lots of cats, and that's what she eats when she runs out of food. Whatever, I try to avoid her.

But with my stomach growling and the food smells overwhelming me, I waited until there was a break in the line and approached.

She's large, with black glasses that make her face look like a cat. She usually wears too much lipstick.

"Hi, Mrs. Garcia," I said, trying to sound as cheery as possible.

She stared at my empty hands. "What do you want?"

"Uh . . ."

"Timberline, right?" she said. "Ashley's brother?"

I nodded, glad she remembered. Everybody likes Ashley. "I was wondering . . ."

"Let me guess," she said, her eyes foggy as mud puddles. "You forgot your money?"

"How'd you know?"

She wrote something on a piece of paper and stuffed it in the cash register. "Three dollars. Pay me tomorrow." When I hesitated, she jerked her head toward the food. "Go on, before I change my mind."

CHAPTER 11

❋ Ashley ❋

When I woke up from my nap, I had missed dinner. Mom kept a plate for me, but I wasn't hungry. She sat on my bed, and we talked.

I cried. I told her I wanted to get better. "I've taken my medicine every day."

"I know," Mom said. "You've done everything we've asked and more."

When Bryce got home he told me about Mrs. Garcia, and I was sorry I had missed it. Everybody thinks she's as mean as a snake, but I've actually gotten her to smile.

"Your principal called," Mom said as I measured out my old medicine and a little of the new. I have to take the pills with food.

"What did Mr. Forster want?"

"The elementary school in Memorial needs tutors after school. He thought you might be interested."

Memorial is a town that's not too far from us. "What would I have to do?"

"Work on math and English. Play games. He suggested you for a second grader."

"You'd have to drive me," I said.

"If it's something you want to do, I don't mind."

Mom knows I want to be a teacher when I grow up. Maybe a special-ed teacher. I told Mr. Forster that the first time Bryce and I met him. He was so kind to us when he found out our dad had been killed.

"I'll do it," I said.

CHAPTER 12

☺ *Bryce* ☺

Sam was on his way out the door to buy a new mailbox when the phone rang. He handed it to me.

"Hi, Bryce," Skeeter said. "Guess what I saw going home on the bus? A bunch of bashed mailboxes."

Skeeter lives closer to the mountains in Red Rock, on the other side of the railroad tracks. The police were right—this wasn't just happening in our area.

"How many?"

"I counted a dozen. They stopped before they got to our house."

"Okay," I said. "See you tomorrow."

Skeeter didn't say anything.

"Did you want something else?" I said.

"Uh . . . is . . . is Ashley home?"

She was at the table taking her medicine. I thought about saying she wasn't available, but I figured this might take her mind off her doctor's visit. "Hang on," I said, and I handed her the phone.

She covered the mouthpiece. "Who is it?"

"Your friend," I said, smiling.

I heard only her end of the conversation, but I could imagine what Skeeter said. Before she hung up, I ran upstairs to my room.

"Bryce!" Ashley screamed through my door. "Why did you have to tell him?"

I was right. For the next half hour I don't think Ashley thought about her doctor's visit once. She was too busy yelling at me about Skeeter.

Finally, I opened the door and explained that the news just slipped out. She threatened to tell Marion Quidley that I wanted to marry her. Marion is an okay girl as girls go, but I'd rather have bamboo shoots jammed under my fingernails than have that rumor spread.

I headed downstairs to get away from Ashley, but she followed me outside. I stopped in the driveway near Randy's truck. He was over studying with Leigh for some big test.

"Look, I don't know how many ways to say it," I said. "I know you don't like Skeeter, and I'll never tell him anything about you again."

Ashley wasn't listening. She was staring at something in the back of Randy's truck.

I turned and looked. In the back was a metal softball bat. I picked it up. It had scratches all over it. On one side I noticed different colors of paint. Just like the paint we had used on our mailbox.

CHAPTER 13

❈ Ashley ❈

I didn't sleep well that night, worrying that my brain might do weird things. When I had my first seizure, my dad found me in Bryce's closet, staring at the ceiling. When I woke up, I knew my name, but I couldn't remember I had a twin brother or my mom's name or our phone number or anything. It was the scariest night of my life.

Now I kept thinking about Randy's bat too, but Bryce said he would look for more clues. Neither of us wanted to get Randy in trouble or to hurt Leigh, but we both knew we had to find the truth.

The next day was Friday, which made me feel better. Something about a weekend helps if you're having a problem. You have time to do stuff you really want to, rather than what everybody says you have to do.

Bryce paid back Mrs. Garcia, the lunch lady, and it went fine. But as I watched her, something seemed wrong. She's mean to kids, snapping at them and giving them looks, but something was different that day. She usually read a book at the cash register, but today she just stared off.

I started toward her when there was no one around, but my friend Hayley got my attention and told me a new family was moving in across the street from her. "And they've got this cute boy who'll be in eighth grade with us next year."

Lunch was almost over when I noticed Mrs. Garcia closing up. I threw away my brown bag and turned, but someone blocked my way.

"Hi, Skeeter," I said.

He was trembling. "I'm really sorry about your sickness."

"Thanks."

"Are you okay now?"

"Yeah . . . I'll be all right."

He held out a square envelope. "I couldn't make it to the store last night."

"Okay," I said.

"I gotta go now. Hope you like the card."

"I'm sure I will." I turned and saw Mrs. Garcia was gone. "I'll read it in my next class."

I walked by Skeeter into the hall and could feel him still looking at me. When I got to my locker, I opened the card. On the front it said *Happy Birthday!* But there was a line through it, and Skeeter had written *Get Well Son.* I guessed he meant *soon.* Inside was a birthday poem, and at the bottom *Love, Mom and Dad* was scratched out and he had signed his name.

Sweet. Low budget, but sweet.

CHAPTER 14

☺ *Bryce* ☺

Randy has a younger brother named Derek in sixth grade. He's short with dark hair and glasses that make him look like a computer geek. I found him outside after lunch and sat beside him.

"I'm Bryce. My sister and your brother are—"

"I know," Derek said.

"How do you like her?"

He shrugged. "Okay for a girl, I guess."

My thoughts exactly. "Who else does Randy hang out with?"

Another shrug. "I guess some guys on his team. He plays in a softball league." He finally looked up at me. "You should come to one of the games. There's one tonight."

"I don't think Leigh would like that."

"Dad makes Randy take me. We could hang out. It'd be fun."

I wasn't so sure, but the chance to snoop around Randy's friends and his house was too good to pass up. "Suggest it to Randy," I said. "Maybe he can talk Leigh into it."

Derek smiled.

CHAPTER 15

✖ Ashley ✖

I told Bryce to go home without me after school. The teachers park in the back near the Dumpsters, and the door the cooks use is back there too. As I'd hoped, I found Mrs. Garcia lifting heavy bags of trash.

"Can I help with that?" I called, taking off my backpack.

She scowled, then realized it was me. "It's okay, Ashley. I have it."

I hadn't realized how strong she was. She lifted the bulging bags into the green bin and slammed the lid.

"Any plans for the weekend?" I said cheerily.

She sighed and leaned against the bin. "Just my other job. I work

Saturday and Sunday this week. Then it's back here on Monday." She headed toward the kitchen, her head down.

I had to ask now or I'd chicken out. "Mrs. Garcia, is something wrong? It's none of my business, but you seemed really down today."

She stopped and turned, like someone was pulling her around with a chain. "How'd you know that?"

I shrugged. "Just seemed like it."

She focused on the ground, and at first she didn't say anything. Then, "Well, you're sharp. I'll give you that." She pulled the hairnet from her head. "Today is sad for me. An anniversary I'd like to forget."

"An anniversary of what?"

"I said I'd like to forget it," she snapped.

Sometimes people say they don't want to talk about things when they really do. But I could tell Mrs. Garcia *really* didn't want to talk about it.

"Okay, have a good weekend," I said, walking away.

She hesitated at the door, then went inside.

CHAPTER 16

◐ *Bryce* ◐

I was playing video games in the exercise room in the barn when Leigh walked in. She doesn't talk to me a lot unless she wants to get me to do her chores. I usually hold out for about twice what the chore is worth and tell her I'm studying to be an economist.

Her look let me know this wasn't about a chore.

She leaned against the wall and crossed her arms. "How did you do it?"

"Do what?"

"Get Derek to ask Randy if you could come tonight?"

I've tried to figure out whether there's a little bit of Leigh that actually likes Ashley, Dylan, and me. I haven't decided yet. Sometimes she's sweet as cotton candy, smiling and giggling at us. Other times she's moody, distant—like a dog that can't make up its mind whether to let you pet it.

I tried to stifle a smile but couldn't. "He wants me to come?"

She rolled her eyes. "Be ready at six or we'll leave without you."

CHAPTER 17

❀ Ashley ❀

As Mom drove me to the school in Memorial for my tutoring job, I asked her about Mrs. Garcia. Mom is in a group of parents who pray for teachers and staff, so I thought she might know something.

"I don't know as much about the cafeteria workers," Mom said, "but I know someone who does. Why?"

"Just wondering."

I used Mom's cell phone to call her friend Mrs. Wilson. She chuckled. "It's nice to hear someone who's not complaining about Mrs. Garcia. Some kids don't even want to go into the cafeteria because of her. She started working here this year. I see her at the bakery on the weekend sometimes. That's her other job. Other than that, I don't know what to tell you."

Mom sends me to the bakery every now and then. I planned how I could run into Mrs. Garcia as Mom parked.

The elementary school was set on the side of a hill with a nice playground in the back. Memorial is an old town the railroad used to run through. There's a lighted star on the side of the hill at Christmas and patriotic days and a big fireworks show there every Fourth of July if it's not too dry.

About 20 little kids and the same number of volunteers showed up, and I got paired with a girl named Angelique. She had big brown eyes and a smile that could melt butter. We played a few games inside, then went to the playground. She said she couldn't read too well and had problems with numbers, so I promised I'd help her.

CHAPTER 18

◌ *Bryce* ◌

Derek and I sat behind Leigh and Randy in Randy's pickup.

I looked around, but I couldn't find anything suspicious. I was hoping to discover a video camera or any clue that Randy was involved in the mailbox vandalism. But would he smash his own girlfriend's mailbox? Maybe someone had borrowed his truck.

"I hear you're still a Cubs fan," Randy said, looking in the rearview mirror. "Think they'll make it to the World Series in our lifetime?"

I chuckled. "Any team can have a bad century."

A sports complex north of us has 10 softball fields, two for soccer, and some playgrounds. Randy carried his cleats and walked in his white socks. A black fence ran around the backstop and dugout area.

Some of the guys on his team were older, and I finally realized this was a church team. "I didn't know Randy went to church," I said to Derek.

"He doesn't. Players have to go at least twice a month during the season, so Randy goes to a Sunday school class where they give you stuff to eat."

A few other players as young as Randy slapped him five. The older guys mostly had bellies Santa would be proud of. They laughed a lot as they threw the ball around.

"Let's go to the concession stand," Derek said.

Leigh dug into her purse and pulled out a five-dollar bill. "Bring me a snow cone."

On the way, I said, "Does Randy let people borrow his truck?"

"Who'd want to?" Derek said, laughing. "I don't think he'd let anybody drive it except Leigh. He treats that thing better than he treats me, even though it's falling apart."

I asked Derek a few more questions, but I soon realized that he didn't know any more about Randy than I did about Leigh.

When the game began, I could have sworn these were two motorcycle clubs playing each other rather than two churches. Guys threw equipment, yelled at the umpire, and one even broke a wooden bat over his leg.

Every time Randy came to the plate, Leigh yelled and clapped for him. I've seen enough baseball to know a good swing. Randy had one right out of a textbook—short step with his front foot, quick hands through the strike zone, and *bam* the ball was gone.

I wondered if Randy would be playing on some prison team if I kept up my investigation.

Randy's team won by three runs, and everybody shook hands. One guy from the other team actually apologized to the umpire in the parking lot.

Randy drove us back to his house so he could take a shower and go to a movie with Leigh. While Leigh talked with Randy's mom, Derek showed me his room. He had a pretty cool video game collection. Even though I don't usually like hanging out with sixth graders, it was fun.

When Derek's mom called him downstairs, I walked into the hallway and heard the shower still running. Randy's room was across the hall, the door open. I crept inside. Little trophies dotted the shelves. The bed wasn't made, and his desk had books piled high.

His DVD collection included a lot of sports movies—*Remember the Titans, Miracle, Hoosiers,* stuff like that. I was about to leave when something caught my eye. Under the bed was a video with something written on the side.

It was one word with several of the letters smudged. It started with *MA,* and ended with an *X.*

Mailbox!

CHAPTER 19

❀ Ashley ❀

As I ate my waffles early Saturday morning, I wondered how I could find out about Mrs. Garcia if she wouldn't talk to me. If it was personal, like a guy leaving her, I was sunk. But if it was a car accident or some other tragedy, maybe it'd be in the files at the newspaper.

Little Dylan came down the stairs with half his car collection stuffed in his pockets. I had to wonder if he'd slept that way. He picked out about five boxes of cereal and some cherry Pop-Tarts. I knew what was going to happen next and didn't need to watch, so I cleaned my plate and went into the living room where I sat at the computer.

I found Mrs. Garcia's first name in our yearbook.

I typed in *Renee Garcia* at the Web site for *The Gazette* in Colorado Springs. Articles popped up with the name *Renee,* but none with *Garcia* as the last name. I checked a couple of the Denver papers too. Nothing.

I was going to have to go to the bakery to get any answers.

CHAPTER 20

◑ *Bryce* ◑

I found Ashley at the computer and told her what I had seen at Randy's the night before.

"Did you watch the video?" Ashley said.

I shook my head. "When that shower turned off, I had to get out of there."

"How do you know it's a video of them smashing mailboxes?"

"I don't. But if we can't find any more clues, we'll have to grab it."

I walked into the kitchen and noticed a list of chores on the blackboard. Mom puts the list up every Friday night, and whoever wakes up earliest gets first pick. Ashley had already picked the easiest—

vacuum living room. The others were clean Dylan's room and doggy cleanup. The last one meant taking a plastic bag out back and picking up dog droppings.

Leigh came up behind me, snatched the chalk from my fingers, and put a check by "Clean Dylan's room."

"Hey, I was going to pick that!" I said.

Leigh slapped the chalk from her hand. "You snooze, you lose."

I gritted my teeth and wanted to yell at her, but then I remembered she was dating a criminal she'd soon be visiting behind bars. Destroying mailboxes is a federal offense—they're actually government property, after all. It made me scared for Randy.

"Have fun last night?" Leigh said.

I nodded. "Interesting game."

"Could you believe the way those players acted?" she said. "That's one reason I don't go to church."

"Because of softball players?"

"They're a bunch of hypocrites," she said. "Praying before the game and then acting like babies during it. The only reason they want Randy to play is because he's good. They don't care about his *soul*." When she said the word *soul*, she made quote marks in the air.

Ashley and I had tried to be nice to Leigh and prayed for her, but she had a habit of knocking church and Christians. Mom told me we needed to love her and not argue, but that was hard.

I wanted to tell her she shouldn't judge all Christians by a few jerks and that calling people hypocrites is an easy way to ignore your own faults.

Instead, I got two plastic bags from under the sink and went on poop patrol.

CHAPTER 21

✽ Ashley ✽

I parked my ATV at Mrs. Watson's house and walked into town to the Black Bear Bakery.

I don't think there's a better smell in the world than fresh bread, unless it's when you mix it with cakes and cookies and pies. I'd pay for a slice of the air in that bakery.

I picked out the cookies I wanted and waited my turn. As the woman at the counter placed them in their own little box, I asked if Mrs. Garcia was still here.

"Went home early," she said. "Don't think she was feeling well."

I decided to take a shortcut behind the bakery back to my ATV, but as I headed that way, another woman caught my eye. She sat on the back steps of the bakery taking long draws from a glass of iced tea. Her hair was as white as wedding cake, her face deeply lined, and her apron had bits of dough stuck to it.

"Excuse me," I said. "Do you know Mrs. Garcia?"

She nodded, eyeing me evenly. "What do you want with Renee?"

"She works at my school. I'm just . . . well, I'm kind of worried about her. She said something about yesterday being the anniversary of something she didn't want to talk about."

The old woman looked like an alligator had jumped out of her tea. She gulped, coughed, then patted her chest. Finally she managed, "You mean the fire?"

"Fire?"

"Years ago, before she moved to Red Rock." She looked away. "If Renee wanted you to know, she would have told you herself."

One thing I've learned is that when people are through telling you something, they're through. You can push, but usually people clam up.

"Where did she live before?"

"Pueblo," the woman said, as if this was her last word.

"Well, thanks," I said.

"You're welcome." She looked a little scared. "But next time ask Renee, and don't tell her I said anything."

CHAPTER 22

☽ *Bryce* ☽

Leigh wasn't dressed up enough to be going out with Randy,
but I didn't want to ask where she was going. When you have an
older sister, sometimes it's better to just try to imagine where she's
going.

"If Randy calls," she said, "tell him I went over to Dawn's. There's
a dance tonight, and she asked me to help with her hair."

I wondered why she and Randy weren't going and how she was
getting to Dawn's, but I didn't ask. She'd only sneer at me.

A car pulled up and honked. Leigh grabbed her purse and some
hair stuff and left.

A few minutes later the phone rang, and it was Randy. "Is Leigh there?"

Randy didn't even acknowledge that I was breathing. Ashley and I called him The Creep, and right then I thought it was pretty accurate. "She went to Dawn's," I told him.

Randy paused. "Do you have that number?"

"Nope. Sorry."

"Well, give her a message," Randy said. I heard someone laugh in the background. "Tell her I can't go out tonight. Something came up. I'll call her tomorrow."

"Okay," I said. "She's going to ask what happened."

"Just tell her it was kind of an emergency."

CHAPTER 23

❀ Ashley ❀

Leigh was upset with Bryce when she got home. I guess he hadn't asked the right questions or something, because she kept asking where Randy had gone. Of course, Bryce had no idea.

I ran upstairs and sat with Bryce on Dylan's bed. "You think we ought to tell somebody what we know about Randy?" Bryce said.

I shook my head. "If you had seen the video, maybe, but we don't really know anything yet. I'd kind of like to believe The Creep wouldn't do something like this."

"What's it going to take to convince you?" Bryce said. "I could go back and get the tape. He's obviously not home tonight."

Dylan just watched us, perched on his bed and yawning. His pillow was lumpy, and I found a bunch of trains stuffed inside. Bryce went out while I sang to Dylan and tucked him in. I guess we had worn him out, because instead of asking a million questions about what we were having for breakfast the next day and wanting more songs, he was snoring within five minutes.

Later, down in the living room, I told Bryce, "We can't accuse Randy of anything until we have proof."

Bryce bit his cheek and took a deep breath. I could tell it was a struggle not to tell me off.

CHAPTER 24

☺ *Bryce* ☺

The next morning I jumped in the shower, then dressed
and went downstairs. Pippin and Frodo scratched at the back door,
and I let them outside and grabbed the paper. I love looking at the
Sunday paper for the comics (the first section I read) and to see
what's coming out on DVD.

In the middle of the Metro section I found a picture of a smashed
mailbox with a sad woman from Red Rock next to it.

Vandalism Causes Heartache

A wave of mailbox vandalism has hit the Red Rock area hard
in the last week. Another round of smashed boxes was
reported last night.

The local postmaster, Arlin Hempkin, said area residents have reported numerous problems in the past few days, with many mailboxes damaged or destroyed.

"My husband and I moved here from Denver to get away from this type of thing," said one resident who wished not to be identified. "People should have more control over their kids."

The article went on to give tips on what to do and not do when repairing a mailbox, but I could only think of one question.

Where had Randy been last night?

CHAPTER 25

✖ Ashley ✖

After church I got an idea about Mrs. Garcia. If she had lived in Pueblo, maybe there was a story in that local newspaper about the fire. On the Internet I found that the Pueblo paper wasn't available online. I racked my brain, then turned to the best source of information I could think of—the local library.

I called and asked for the reference department. A lady answered, and I said I was looking for information about a fire in Pueblo that had happened in the last few years. I gave her the date and Mrs. Garcia's name. I said she could just send it via e-mail if she found anything.

Suddenly I felt a little hope that I'd find out the truth about Mrs. Garcia.

CHAPTER 26

◎ *Bryce* ◎

Ashley rode ahead of me to school the next day, and as we
pulled up to Mrs. Watson's barn I noticed something strange in her
front yard. She has one of those cheap plastic mailboxes with the little flag that never goes up right. The mailbox was gone, and black
stuff ran down the metal pole. A black wire covered with plastic lay
at the bottom.

"Looks like a sparkler," I said.

Mrs. Watson came out in her robe, and I showed her the mailbox.
"That must have been what Peanuts was barking at last night," she
said. "He was going crazy around midnight. Guess those hooligans

have been at it again. This used to be such a nice little town. You could leave your doors unlocked. Now I have to keep my pistol loaded."

"You really have a gun?" Ashley said.

"Second Amendment, my dear."

We'd studied the right to bear arms in school. Half the class thought everybody should have guns, and the other half thought nobody should have them. "Guns don't kill people," somebody said. "People kill people."

I pictured Mrs. Watson and a group from the sewing circle at church organizing a militia of gray-haired ladies. Maybe there would be fewer smashed mailboxes.

"Bryce, could you and your dad help me put up a new mailbox?"

"Sure."

At school Randy's little brother, Derek, was near the flagpole with a bunch of his friends.

"How's your brother?" I said.

"Okay, I guess."

"What happened to him Saturday night? He said it was kind of an emergency."

Derek shrugged. "He went out with a bunch of his friends from the softball team, I think."

CHAPTER 27

✖ Ashley ✖

I raced home to look at my e-mail, but Leigh was on the computer. "Wait your turn," she said.

After I put my stuff away she was still there, listening to music as she read. I wanted to see if the library had found anything. All I had to do was copy it to a disk and take it to the computer downstairs.

Leigh moved like a glacier, and Mom was no help. "She'll be done in a minute," she whispered. I had heard the saying "walking on eggshells," but this was the first time I knew what it meant.

When she finally clicked off the music and swished out of the room, I found I had three new messages. One from Marion Quidley said she thought all the bashed mailboxes were *space aliens trying to tell us something!* Another was from my friend Hayley and didn't have much to do with anything at all.

And there was one from the Pueblo Public Library. *Attached please find a copy of the article I discovered in a local paper from seven years ago.*

Apartment Fire Claims One

An infant was killed in an apartment fire late last night on South Pueblo Boulevard. Officials say the blaze began in the infant's bedroom and was contained there.

Six-month-old Danielle Garcia was in the care of a babysitter at the time of the fire. Officials did not release the babysitter's name. Danielle's mother, Renee Garcia, was working at the time. Upon hearing the news she collapsed and was rushed to the hospital.

Neighbors described Ms. Garcia as a devoted mother. "She was just trying to earn a living and bring up her child," one said. "This tears my heart out."

Officials say the cause of the fire is still under investigation.

CHAPTER 28

☯ *Bryce* ☯

Sam and I went to Mrs. Watson's house later that day to put up a new mailbox.

"Think the same people did this?" I said. "The mailboxes up the street look like they were blown up with cherry bombs and sparklers, but none of them was smashed."

Sam nodded. "Could be the same people using different methods. Fireworks is a little higher class—don't you think?"

I thought about Randy and his softball buddies. "What could happen to these people if they get caught?"

"A big fine and something like three years in prison for each offense."

That took my breath away. "They must have hit 20 mailboxes on our road alone," I said.

Sam cocked his head at me. "You know something about this?"

I shook my head. "Ashley and I are just trying to figure it out."

Sam scrunched his mouth and bit his cheek. "I've ordered a surveillance camera for the house. You could use it, but don't take any chances. These guys find out you're after them, who knows what they might do."

CHAPTER 29

❀ Ashley ❀

Losing a baby in a fire had to be the worst thing that could happen to a mother. At lunch the next day I looked for a chance to talk with Mrs. Garcia, but she was busy the whole time. She smiled at me as I went through the line, but that was it.

I saw our principal, Mr. Forster, outside his office during a class change.

"Can I ask you a question about Mrs. Garcia?"

He squinted at me and nodded slowly, as if I could ask but he might not answer.

"I heard what happened to her a few years ago. Do you know why she moved here?"

Mr. Forster looked away, then motioned me back into the main office. "Has she been mean to you?" he said as we walked.

"No, I've just been talking with her a little. Finding out stuff."

He frowned. "I don't normally talk with students about the staff. If something happens with one of our employees, I want to hear about it, of course. Mrs. Garcia has problems like all of us. This is her third school in the last three years. Some think she shouldn't be working with the students because of her demeanor. She's working on it. And she's a hard worker, always on time."

"Do you think she'll be at our school next year?"

From the way he looked at me I knew the conversation was over.

CHAPTER 30

☺ *Bryce* ☺

At youth group Wednesday night, our leader, Pastor Andy, brought a bunch of watermelons and cut them in three pieces each. We were supposed to use a spoon and create something out of what was left.

I thought I'd just scoop the whole thing out and wear it as a hat, but the more I dug around the edges, the more it looked like a mountain. So I kept going and soon had the likeness of Pikes Peak, which I thought would win.

Wrong. Second place went to a sixth grade boy who carved a 747 (his dad's a pilot), and first place went to an eighth grade girl who created the image of Abraham Lincoln, complete with the mole on his right cheek.

Show-offs. These were serious watermelon artists.

Then we all went outside and gathered around a big hunk of wood. A man wearing plastic goggles started a chainsaw and moved quickly around the wood, kicking out chips that covered the ground. When he was done, he stepped back and we all gasped. The block of wood had become a beautiful owl sitting on a perch.

Pastor Andy's point was to show us what even something ordinary can become in the hands of an artist. He encouraged us to give our lives to God, the Artist of the universe, and let him shape us into something great.

Somehow during his talk I figured out how we could catch the mailbox bashers. Randy or not, they had to be caught.

CHAPTER 31

❀ Ashley ❀

I cornered Pastor Andy after the meeting. He has a goofy-looking face with short hair and big ears, but he really cares about kids and we all like him.

Andy has a way of focusing on you and what you're talking about instead of thinking about the next thing he has to clean up or who else he has to talk to.

"What's the best way to get a person to open up about their life?" I said.

He raised his eyebrows. "Good question. Who are we talking about?"

Andy looked surprised when I told him. He probably thought I was interested in some guy.

"If you've become her friend," he said, "which it sounds like you have, that's a great first step. People are a lot more open if you share something personal too. If they sense they can trust you, they're more likely to talk. Now let me ask you something."

"Sure."

"Ashley, is something bothering you? You seem kind of upset or antsy."

"What do you mean?" I said, my face feeling hot.

"You're not your usual self. You look kind of serious."

I thought about the change in medicine and what the doctor had said. All I could do was shrug, and thankfully, Pastor Andy didn't press me.

CHAPTER 32

☺ *Bryce* ☺

Mom said no to my idea so fast my head almost spun around. "You're not sleeping outside on a school night. Besides, it's dangerous with all the stuff going on."

I let it drop, then went to Sam. This guy had lived a dangerous life and had admitted to us that in the army he had been trained to kill people. If anybody could talk Mom into letting us investigate another mystery, it was Sam.

"I agree with your mother," Sam said. "But wait until the weekend, and I'll put the camper on the back of my truck. You'll be safer there."

Thursday morning I took a can of red spray paint and a piece of paper out to our mailbox and created my own masterpiece.

"Looks like a target," Ashley said.

"You got it," I said.

CHAPTER 33

Ashley

We got out of fourth period early for lunch because our teacher had a meeting, and the cafeteria was nearly empty. It was the perfect chance to talk with Mrs. Garcia.

I sat with my brown bag and watched as she spoke with the cooks. She finally came to the cash register when a wave of students washed through. I got in line.

"How's Ashley today?" she said.

"You want the truth or just the smile?"

She looked at me over her glasses. "The truth."

I sighed. "The truth is, I'm on some new medicine for this seizure thing I have, and it's hard to get used to. It kind of scares me."

"Seizures?"

I explained and she listened closely.

"I had no idea," she said.

"It's a bummer, but the doctor says I can still grow out of it."

She asked about the medicine and whether it hurts my stomach. I also told her about the EEGs and that Bryce and I stay up late before my appointments.

The bell rang and the stampede headed our way. I leaned close and whispered, "I found out about your daughter. I'm really sorry."

The blood drained from her face. "How?"

"Newspapers. I didn't mean to snoop."

Her eyes darted around the room as other kids made their way through the food line. She looked like a scared child.

"If you ever want to talk about it—"

She stopped me with one look, and at first I thought I had gone too far. But she said, "After school. Can you stay?"

CHAPTER 34

☺ *Bryce* ☺

I found Randy's brother, Derek, and bragged about the target on our mailbox. I hoped he would tell Randy. All the clues pointed to him, but I couldn't limit my investigation to just one suspect, especially when I wasn't sure. I decided to approach the meanest group at school, led by none other than Boo Heckler.

Ashley and I had a run-in with Boo, who had threatened us if we didn't let him ride our ATVs. I had stood up to him, which felt good, and Boo hadn't bothered us since.

He sat with a few friends in the shade behind the school. They're all tobacco challenged. By the time kids get to be our age, everybody knows the dangers of smoking, but I guess Boo and his gang don't care. They smell like ashtrays. It's hard to even breathe around them.

Boo looked up like I was holding a fire extinguisher, threatening to put out their smokes. "What do you want, Timberline?"

"Got something funny for you. With all the mailbox bashing, we've painted a target on ours."

Boo paused, took a puff, and looked at his friends. "I'm holding my sides."

Everybody laughed.

Then I told as many people as I could who might have friends or relatives who could be the vandals.

And I hoped they wouldn't come back until Friday night.

CHAPTER 35

✖ Ashley ✖

When the final bell rang I raced to the lunchroom and found Mrs. Garcia sitting on one of the tall kitchen stools by the garbage bins out back. Her back was to me, and I could tell she was crying by the way her shoulders shook. She turned when I put my backpack down. Her eyes were red and her face splotchy. You don't think of grown-ups crying like little kids, but Mrs. Garcia looked like she was about four years old.

She wiped her face and blew her nose. "Tell me what you found out about Danielle."

I told her what I'd read in the newspaper and she said, "You'd better sit down."

I sat on my backpack in the smelly air around the garbage bins. You don't find a lot of flies in our part of Colorado, but it looked like they were having a convention behind the school.

Mrs. Garcia watched a bus winding its way from the school into Red Rock. "She would have been seven now, finishing second grade."

"How did it happen?" I said.

"Danielle was only a few weeks old when John, my husband, shipped out with the army from Fort Carson. I didn't want to leave Danielle, but we needed the money. I worked nights when it was easier to get a sitter.

"A young woman in the neighborhood—a teacher named Tonya Zoloff—was pregnant and offered to watch Danielle for free. Said it would be good training."

Mrs. Garcia wiped her eyes again. "While I was walking home from work at about 10 that night, I heard the sirens and saw the lights. When I saw smoke coming from our building, I could hardly breathe. Firemen were shooting water into our apartment.

"I raced upstairs, and one of the neighbors said, 'There she is.' Tonya was wrapped in a blanket, an oxygen mask over her face. I lifted the blanket, looking for Danielle, but she wasn't there. That's when I started screaming.

"I passed out and came to in the hospital. I found out the baby-sitter had fallen asleep on the couch after putting Danielle to bed. When she woke up, she smelled smoke and ran to Danielle's room. When Tonya opened the door, she said it was like the whole room exploded. She was able to dial 911 from the kitchen and then ran outside."

"She never got to Danielle?"

Mrs. Garcia shook her head and looked up, as if she could still see the scene. "I'll never forget finally going home and seeing her room. I'd found a border with animals and Noah's ark. It was so bright and cheery. But now her little crib was as black as coal, the walls torn up, plaster hanging, water damage everywhere. We had the funeral with no body."

"*No* body? How could that be?"

"The firefighters said Danielle must have been consumed. And because she was a newborn, there wasn't even any bone tissue left."

The whole thing creeped me out. I couldn't believe they couldn't find any trace of the baby, but if the firefighters said it was true . . .

"How did the fire start?" I said.

"They said the electrical connection to the baby monitor was frayed and had probably sparked."

"I'll bet the babysitter felt awful."

Mrs. Garcia nodded. "She moved away a few days later, and I haven't seen her since. I think she just felt too bad. A month later my husband was killed in a roadside bombing. I was all alone."

Mrs. Garcia leaned forward. "Ashley, I don't think my baby died that night."

CHAPTER 36

◑ *Bryce* ◑

All the mailboxes on our road had been fixed except one—
and those people were on vacation. I hoped the news about my target mailbox had made the rounds.

When I got home, Randy's truck was in the driveway. I saw a
huge plastic bag in the backseat. It had red, white, and blue wrap-
pers inside.

"What're you looking at?" Leigh said as she and Randy walked up.

I just about dropped my backpack. "Oh! Uh . . . n-nothing. I
m-mean, what's in the bag?"

"My dad got me some fireworks," Randy said. "Firecrackers and
stuff."

"Cool," I said. "Got any cherry bombs?"
"Yeah."
"How about sparklers?"
"Sure."

CHAPTER 37

✾ Ashley ✾

Mrs. Garcia held out a picture. "This is my Danielle."

"She's beautiful," I said.

"Every time I see a bus go by or those milk cartons with missing children's faces on them, I think about my baby. I've been working at different schools the past few years, hoping, praying . . ."

"You've been looking for her?"

She nodded and stared at the ground.

"Why do you think she's still alive?"

"The window was open," Mrs. Garcia said. "The firemen said it was like that when they arrived. I never got to ask Tonya, but it was cold that evening and I'm sure she wouldn't have opened it. I think someone took my baby and set the fire to make it look like she had been killed."

I went straight to my room when I got home, lit my candle, and opened my diary. I wrote everything I could remember about what Mrs. Garcia told me, including the babysitter's full name—I guessed at the spelling. Before dinner, I ran a search on the Internet but turned up nothing for Tonya Zoloff.

I knew it had to be hard for Mrs. Garcia to admit her baby was dead, but if there was a chance she could be alive, I had to help her.

CHAPTER 38

☺ *Bryce* ☺

Everybody was excited at dinner because Leigh was taking her driver's test the next day. She was going out later to finish her night hours with Sam. To get your license you have to do a lot of driving with your parents in the car, I guess.

That night, I kept peeking out the window from the second-floor hallway, watching our mailbox through the pine trees in front of the house. I wished Mom and Sam would let me spend the night camping out, but this was the next best thing to being there.

Ashley hadn't said much at dinner, and I could tell something was bothering her. The past few days she had acted weird. I wondered if it was her medicine.

I woke up propped against the window, with Pippin and Frodo barking. It was as dark as a Hershey's bar outside. Two headlights stared at me from the end of our driveway. I grabbed Sam's night-vision scope.

It was a car with something written on the side. A police car. As it pulled away, the two cops were talking, pointing at my target, and smiling.

CHAPTER 39

✖ Ashley ✖

In art class the next day, our teacher, Mr. Cheplosa, turned on a new computer program. We had been learning about drawing faces. "With this I can actually scan your picture and show you what you might look like in 10 or 20 or even 50 years."

The class giggled, and Skeeter hurried up front with one of our yearbooks. "Mr. Cheplosa, why don't you scan Ashley?"

"Great," Mr. Cheplosa said.

Before I could protest, kids around me laughed and clapped, saying, "Yeah, Ashley!"

He scanned in the photo and brought up my picture. I could feel my face turn red as my face seemed to fill the screen. Split ends. Ugh. And I thought of all the things I wanted to do to Skeeter after school, like run over him with my ATV or rip his dumb birthday/get well card into a billion pieces.

"Now," Mr. Cheplosa said, "here's what she'll look like in 10 years."

The second picture was of Mickey Mouse, and the rest of the class acted like it was the funniest thing in the world.

Mr. Cheplosa put my real picture back on the screen and blew my face up really big.

"It's the monster that ate Red Rock!" somebody said.

Skeeter gazed at the screen and smiled. I imagined him with a big tire print on his forehead. It wasn't what Jesus would have thought, but I couldn't help it.

"Okay, quiet down," Mr. Cheplosa said, focusing on the computer. "Now this is what Ashley might look like in high school."

My face morphed. My hair was straight, a little shorter, and white teeth gleamed. A little makeup would have helped, but I actually looked pretty.

"Extreme makeover!" a guy hollered.

"And here's college," Mr. Cheplosa said.

My face was thinner, and my eyes had a few lines. It was exciting to see but kind of scary too.

"And here's what she'll look like on her 75th birthday." Mr. Cheplosa glanced at me. "You ready for this?"

An old woman with gray hair and wrinkled skin filled the screen, but I could tell it was me.

The bell rang and I was glad. Then I got an idea. A great idea.

CHAPTER 40

◕ *Bryce* ◕

While I ate, Ashley went up to the Lunch Lady and talked for a long time.

Duncan sat beside me and nodded toward them. "What's that all about?"

I shrugged.

On the way to our next classes Ashley clutched a small picture and had a look in her eye like she had just aced a test or performed the perfect dance routine.

The picture was of a baby with a bow in her hair. By the time we got to the art room, Ashley had told me all about it, and I was as excited as she was at what we might find out.

CHAPTER 41

❈ Ashley ❈

Mr. Cheplosa was in his darkroom. I couldn't imagine why anyone would want to develop photos when you can do it digitally, but Mr. Cheplosa says photography is an art and he likes the old-fashioned way.

I handed him the photo. "Can you make her a few years older, like, say, seven?"

He winced. "Do you have anything larger that doesn't have these creases?"

I shook my head. "Can we try it?"

He placed the photo on the scanner. "This works best with bigger photos and older subjects, so no guarantees. What's this for?"

I looked at Bryce. "This baby died in a fire. I just wanted to show her mom what she might look like now."

Mr. Cheplosa stopped. "Are you sure? Won't this upset the mother?"

I shook my head again. "It was a long time ago."

Mr. Cheplosa clicked the mouse and the computer whirred. An error message came up and my heart sank. He frowned. "It's not reading the photo. You sure your friend doesn't have a better one?"

"Let me check."

I ran to the lunchroom, with only five minutes before my next class. One of the cooks said Mrs. Garcia was on her break. "Try the teachers' lounge."

Great. The other end of school.

I hurried there and knocked on the door.

One of the science teachers stuck his head out and scowled like I had interrupted some big experiment.

"Is Mrs. Garcia in there?"

He looked at the name on the door. "If I'm not mistaken, this is the teachers' lounge. Is she a teacher?"

"No, but someone said—"

"Then I suggest you look elsewhere."

"But this is really important—"

I looked past him as he shut the door, then scanned the hallway. "Mrs. Garcia?" I called. Kids milled around, opening and closing lockers. They stared at me, and I jumped as the bell rang.

CHAPTER 42

☺ *Bryce* ☺

The art room started to fill, and when Ashley didn't return, I headed to my next period.

In the middle of class I looked out the window and saw Mrs. Garcia walking toward the front of the building. I raised my hand and asked if I could go to the restroom. I did have to go, by the way.

I got a pass and headed down the hall. I didn't see Mrs. Garcia anywhere, and as I neared the office, Mr. Forster stepped out.

"Looking for someone, Mr. Timberline?" the principal said.

I showed him my bathroom pass, and he pointed back the way I had come. When I reached the bathroom door I looked back. Mr. Forster smiled and waved like royalty.

When I came out he was gone, so I checked the hallway again. Mrs. Garcia was at the other end. I tried to call her, but she made it around the corner before I could get her attention.

I had to make a quick decision, because if my teacher found out I was running the halls I'd be in trouble. I figured if we helped Mrs. Garcia it would be okay.

I didn't catch her until she was past the gym. "Do you have another picture of your daughter?" I said, trying to catch my breath. "Anything bigger?"

"At home," she said.

"Could you get it before school is over?"

She looked at her watch. "I suppose, if you think it would help."

CHAPTER 43

✖ Ashley ✖

Just before the final bell rang at the end of the day, Mrs. Garcia gave our teacher an envelope. The teacher handed it to me as everyone left the room.

I couldn't wait to look at it, but I had to. Bryce and I pushed through the crowds in the hall.

Skeeter came up beside me. "Hope you didn't mind that I suggested your picture in art."

I gritted my teeth and just stared ahead. The whole thing had given me a good idea, but I didn't want to tell Skeeter.

"She'll get over it," Bryce said.

When we finally made it to the art room, I found a substitute wiping off the blackboard and gathering drawings. "Where's Mr. Cheplosa?

"Doctor's appointment. Back Monday."

Monday. How can I wait until Monday?

CHAPTER 44

☺ *Bryce* ☺

Ashley was really upset about missing Mr. Cheplosa, so I tried to take her mind off it by asking her to tell me everything she knew about the case. It was strange that no one believed the baby was still alive except the mom.

Ashley helped me carry my stuff to Sam's truck for my campout and asked if I wanted company. "I can sleep tomorrow," she said.

I was glad, because as much as I wanted to be out spying, I didn't really want to be alone.

Sam pulled into the driveway with Leigh, and it looked like they had both been to a funeral. He had hardly stopped when Leigh jumped out and raced inside.

"Did she pass her driving test?" I called out.

Sam frowned and shook his head. "She was doing fine until a dog ran in front of her."

"Oh no," Ashley said.

"Missed the dog but hit the curb. Flat tire. Instructor had to get out and change it. It wasn't a pleasant drive home, if you know what I mean."

"At least she didn't run over the dog," Ashley said.

Sam sighed. "Yeah, but somebody else did a few minutes later. Leigh saw the whole thing."

"How awful," Ashley said.

Some people say everything happens for a reason. Like maybe Leigh flunked her driver's test because God knew she would plunge off a cliff the next day if she was driving. But if that was true, why didn't God do something to keep my dad from getting on his plane the day he died?

Randy drove up and got out with a bouquet of flowers.

"Might want to hold off on those," Sam said.

CHAPTER 45

✳ Ashley ✳

Mom had balloons and a congratulations banner strung across the dining-room entry, not to mention a cake in the shape of a car. Bryce whispered, "Good thing Mom didn't make it in the shape of a mailbox or you-know-who would have smashed it by now."

Mom told Randy that Leigh was too upset to talk and that she would call him later. Randy said he understood and gave Mom the flowers, which was nice. Maybe I'd tell that to the judge if Randy went to trial.

"You can tell her I didn't pass my first test," Randy said. "I don't think she knows that."

"I will," Mom said, smiling.

I followed Mom upstairs and stood outside Leigh's door. It was open a crack so I could hear.

"I don't really care about the stupid license," she sobbed. "It's just that . . ."

"What?" Mom said.

Leigh groaned. "It's times like this that I miss Mom the most. Not that you're not doing a good job—"

"I understand," Mom said.

"I just wish she hadn't gotten on that plane. She said she'd always be there for me, and now she's not."

That was how I felt about my dad. Sam was nice, but he wasn't my real dad. A tear trickled down my cheek as I listened. Then I went to my room.

I wished I could say something to Leigh that would convince her that God was real, he cared about how much she hurt, and he wanted her to know him. But she seemed so closed to God, the Bible, and everything I believed.

There were times when I'd be sitting in church, listening to what the pastor or somebody else said, and I'd think, "I wish Leigh could hear this right now."

But the more I prayed that God would break through, the less Leigh seemed to be interested.

I try to have some sort of devotional each day, whether from a book or reading the Bible. The reading from my devotional that day was from Ephesians, chapter 5. "Imitate God, therefore, in everything you do, because you are his dear children. Live a life filled with love, following the example of Christ. He loved us and offered himself as a sacrifice for us, a pleasing aroma to God."

I pulled out my diary and wrote:

God, other than praying for Leigh, I'm not sure there's anything I can say that will help change her. I want to live a life of love for her and show her that you change people. Open her eyes and help me to be a good example for her, even when she really ticks me off.

CHAPTER 46

◒ *Bryce* ◒

As soon as the sun went down it got cold. I was glad Ashley and I were in the truck camper and not in a tent. There are no lights on our country road. Just the stars and the moon.

The batteries in my walkie-talkie were weak, but I figured there was enough juice to reach the house if I had to.

"What are you going to do with the picture of that girl if Mr. Cheplosa can age it?" I said.

Ashley peered into the darkness with the night-vision scope. "Maybe send it to the newspaper, make some flyers, stuff like that. There's got to be a way to find her "

"And you think the girl is alive?"

She shrugged. "All I know is that that open window bothers me. And it makes no sense that there wouldn't be something left of the baby, even if she was burned. Those TV shows find DNA left over at every crime scene. Why not this one?"

"The firefighters and the cops investigated, Ash. They're probably right."

"Probably. But it won't hurt to ask questions."

CHAPTER 47

❋ Ashley ❋

I finally got into a comfortable position in the back of the truck. We had two air mattresses smushed up against the side. We finally moved them so I could lean against the wheel well and still see outside.

We played war for an hour with Bryce's glow-in-the-dark cards. Bryce really gets into it, and it makes me laugh when I win.

In the middle of a game, he said, "Do you think Dad can see us from heaven?"

Interesting question when you're playing war. "I don't know. Why?"

"Some say dead people become angels and watch over them. I like to think Dad can see us and even help us."

"You know people don't become angels," I said. "People are people and angels are angels. They don't switch when they die. And angels don't die anyway."

"I know, but if Dad can't see us, he's going to miss us growing up and graduating and stuff like that. I bet he'd love watching us ride our ATVs."

I had thought a lot about Dad being able to see us. Especially when I cried myself to sleep at night. Sometimes I'd imagine his voice, reading to me before I went to sleep. The first months after he died I could see him sitting there, rubbing my back with one hand as he held the book in the other. Now I had to look at his picture on my nightstand just to remember his face.

"Dad probably sees a lot more than we think," I said.

Bryce sat up. He looked like something had just stung him. "God knows everything, right?"

"If he doesn't, we're in big trouble."

"He must know if this girl is alive, and *if* she is, *where* she is."

"Yeah. 'Course."

"Let's ask him to help us find her."

Now I sat up. "Or give us a sign in case she's already in heaven."

Bryce nodded.

"You go first," I said.

"Okay." Bryce closed his eyes. "Dear God, Ash and I need your help again. Thanks for answering our prayers about Boo Heckler and my math test the other day. But now we need to know about a little girl named . . ."

"Danielle."

"... Yeah. We don't even know if she's alive, or if her mom is just hoping, but if she *is* alive, could you help us find her?"

It was my turn. I prayed that Mr. Cheplosa would be there Monday and "that you'd help us use the picture to find her if she's alive."

An engine revved and tires crunched gravel. I opened my eyes to two headlights shining into the back of the truck.

CHAPTER 48

◎ *Bryce* ◎

Ashley and I ducked and stayed down. I thought we'd been spotted, but whoever it was kept coming slowly. Finally the vehicle turned into our driveway, and its lights went out.

"Who is it?" Ashley whispered.

"How should I know?" My heart pounded as a door opened, then closed.

Through the night-shot feature on my video camera I saw someone walk toward the house carrying something. I hit the Record button, thinking maybe the vandals were getting braver.

I scanned the back of the truck to look at the license plate, but it was parked sideways. The night shot made everything look green, so I couldn't even tell the color of the truck. It looked just as beat-up as Randy's though.

Ashley grabbed the walkie-talkie.

"Wait," I said. "Someone's on the porch, putting something by the door."

"What if it's a bomb?" Ashley said. She keyed the mike. "Sam, can you hear me?" Pause. "Sam, are you there?"

No response. *C'mon, Sam!*

"It's Randy," I said, straining to see his lanky body trudging back to the truck empty-handed.

"You sure?" Ashley said. "What's he doing here?"

"Maybe he came back to smash more than just our mailbox," I said.

When Randy neared his truck, Ashley keyed the mike again. "Sam, it's okay. Randy just left something. Probably for Leigh. Do you copy?"

I grabbed the walkie-talkie. "Batteries are shot. You want to go inside?"

"No, do you?"

I shook my head.

As Randy pulled away, Ashley said, "Come on, let's see what it is."

CHAPTER 49

Ashley

The grass was wet on my socks as Bryce and I stole back to the house. Pippin and Frodo growled from inside, and we shushed them.

A basket covered in plastic sat near the door. Inside was fruit, a small pack of homemade brownies, a box of chocolates, and other candy. A card with *Leigh* written on the envelope was taped to the plastic.

"Should we open it?" Bryce said.

I rolled my eyes. "You don't know anything about love."

After we raced back to the truck, I was so tired I went to sleep. I woke up cold, and it was still pitch-black outside.

Bryce was staring out at the road. "I can't believe Randy didn't come back to smash our mailbox."

"You can't be sure Randy's involved in that." I yawned.

"All the clues point to him," Bryce said, putting his video camera away. "Plus, it would look suspicious if every mailbox on our road was smashed except ours."

"Maybe we'll catch him tomorrow night," I said.

CHAPTER 50

○ *Bryce* ○

I woke Ashley at sunup, and we went in to our own beds. I got up a couple of hours later, just as Leigh was coming down the stairs. I wanted to tell her I was sorry about the driving test, sorry about the dog, sorry I hadn't been a better brother, but all I said was, "Randy brought you something last night."

She stared at me. "Were you spying on him?"

"No, we just happened to see him."

Leigh rolled her eyes. I guess lots of big sisters do that to little brothers, but it makes me want to put slimy things in her bed. "What is it?" she said, hustling down the stairs.

Leigh rushed to the dining-room table to look at her basket. Mom was on the phone, but she smiled at Leigh. I could tell something had changed between them. Something good.

Mom turned back to the phone. "Ashley just doesn't seem herself. She's tired and irritable." I realized Mom was talking to the doctor. "I haven't heard anything from her teachers, but I can check. . . ."

Mom made an appointment to take Ashley back in the next week, and I had a sinking feeling that more was going on than I wanted to know.

CHAPTER 51

Ashley

I usually went two or three months between doctor's visits. Mom hugged me, kissed me on top of the head, and said everything was going to be all right, but I wasn't convinced.

Bryce got invited to a sleepover, so I called Hayley and asked if she wanted to camp out with me that night. Maybe I could get her to go to church with me in the morning.

As soon as Hayley arrived that evening, I grabbed some drinks and she pulled a bag of popcorn from the microwave. Then we headed for the truck. We also took a portable TV with a DVD player that hooks into the cigarette lighter, so we settled into our sleeping bags and started watching the second Lord of the Rings movie. When it got scary, I brought Pippin and Frodo out to sleep with us. It was hard to keep them away from the popcorn.

The truck battery must have gotten low because a bunch of squiggly lines appeared on the TV and Gollum looked like he had five legs instead of two. Finally the thing quit on us, so we just talked. Hayley brought up Duncan Swift and said she knew I liked him.

"He doesn't even know I exist. He probably likes you. The only boy I know who likes me is Skeeter Messler, and I wish he didn't."

She asked about my doctor's visits. I told her I was nervous because they'd asked me to come back in so soon, but I added, "I'm just really trying to trust God about it."

"I wish I could believe as strongly as you do. Sometimes I don't even know if I believe God's up there, with all the bad stuff that happens."

"The more bad stuff that happens, the more sure I am that he's there," I said. "Sometimes he's the only thing we can really hold on to."

"What's he like? I mean, what do you think he's like?"

I remembered the scene in *Anne of Green Gables* when Marilla asks Anne if she knows who God is. Anne says, "God is a spirit, infinite, eternal and unchangeable, in His being, wisdom, power, holiness, justice, goodness, and truth." But I knew Hayley didn't need to hear that. What would she think?

Before I could come up with a good answer, Hayley said, "I'm scared about dying and not knowing what happens afterward. Do you ever get scared of that?"

I nodded. "You wouldn't be human if you didn't. But that's one of the best things about Jesus. . . ." As soon as that one name came out of my mouth, the whole mood changed. It was like *abracadabra* to a magician. I mentioned Jesus, and it was as if someone pulled the clouded-eye bunny out of Hayley's hat. I tried to tell her that Jesus took away the fear of death because we could be sure of going to heaven, but it was obvious she had stopped listening.

She said she was tired and turned over in her sleeping bag, her back to me.

I prayed silently that God would help me say something that would grab Hayley's attention.

CHAPTER 52

☺ *Bryce* ☺

Kael's parents have a small house with only three bed-
rooms, but downstairs they have a pool table, air hockey, and a big-
screen TV. We put down our sleeping bags and started to play pool.

"I get the winner," Duncan said as he ran down the stairs. I didn't
even know he was coming, but it was okay.

We played cutthroat pool and a couple of other games before
Kael's mom took us to the video store and to pick up some pizza.

We wandered the aisles looking at movies. One person would
suggest a video, and the other two would shout it down as lame or
too much of a girl movie.

We had moved to the action/adventure section when Kael pecked me on the shoulder and pointed. "Isn't that your sister?"

Leigh stood outside with Randy, talking to a police officer on the sidewalk. The officer pointed to Randy's truck, and Randy said something. Finally the officer walked away, and Randy and Leigh came inside the store.

Leigh looked surprised—and I think disappointed—to see me. I waved, and Randy smiled that what-are-you-doing-here-little-kid? smile. I told them I was here to find a movie, and they went to the comedy section.

On the way back to Kael's, Duncan said, "What did that cop want with your sister and her boyfriend?"

I shrugged. But of course I knew.

CHAPTER 53

❈ Ashley ❈

I woke up groggy with something crawling over me. It was Frodo, and his little claws sank into my skin. I yelled for him to stop, but he wouldn't. I grabbed him, and he was shaking all over. I could feel his little heart beating through his rib cage. Pippin whined at the back of the truck, pressing against the window.

"What is it, boy?" I said.

Hayley was still sound asleep, and it was dark outside.

Then I heard it.

The rev of an engine. Headlights flashed along the side of the truck camper. I fumbled in the dark for Bryce's camera.

The vehicle sped up and seemed to be heading right for us. The lights got brighter and brighter, and I saw the reflection of something in the corner. *The camera!* I turned it on but everything was fuzzy—the dogs had licked the lens.

I quickly tried to wipe it with my shirt. The lights were close now, and someone whooped. Hayley sat up and screamed, light streaming through her hair.

I pointed the camera just as I heard the sickening sound of our new mailbox leaving this world. I zoomed in on the truck, but my hands were shaking so much that I couldn't focus. Pippin and Frodo must have thought the world was coming to an end because they cowered.

"What was that?" Hayley said.

"Bryce's plan worked. But he's going to kill me for falling asleep."

CHAPTER 54

○ *Bryce* ○

It wasn't Ashley's fault that she missed the action. We tried to watch the tape, but the auto-focus feature didn't react quickly enough in the darkness. All she got was a mess of motion through a dark, streaky lens and Pippin and Frodo whimpering.

After church Sunday I went with Sam to the hardware store to pick out a new mailbox. I couldn't believe how big the one was that he picked, and then he also chose a smaller one.

"Which one are you going to get?" I said.

"Both."

"Why?"

"You'll see."

Sam also put a heavy bag of concrete in the cart. I couldn't imagine what he was going to do.

Back at the house, he had me take a bucket of water and the wheelbarrow to the garage. When I got there, he had the big mailbox on the ground, facing up.

He mixed the concrete in the wheelbarrow, put the smaller mailbox inside the big one, and poured the concrete around it.

Sam is a strong guy, but it took everything he had to wheel his invention out to the street and lift the thing onto the post.

"I don't get it," I said.

"The guy swinging the bat will," Sam said. "It'll be like trying to smash granite with a toothpick."

"Okay if I paint another target?" I said.

Sam smiled. "Put one on both sides this time."

CHAPTER 55

❦ Ashley ❦

I was looking at Danielle's baby picture Sunday afternoon when Mom walked into my room. "Who's that?"

The whole story tumbled out like she had opened the door to a stuffed closet.

"Why do you think she hasn't tried to find Danielle before now?" she said.

"I don't think she knows where to start."

"Is Bryce helping with this?"

I nodded and told her about Mr. Cheplosa's computer program and what we hoped to do with the new photo.

Mom looked at the floor and took a breath. I could tell she was trying to think of what to say that wouldn't hurt my feelings.

"What?" I said. "You don't like us investigating this?"

"Ash, I don't want to dampen your enthusiasm, but don't get your hopes up, okay? Sometimes people . . . well, sometimes they have a hard time letting go of things."

"You think Mrs. Garcia is crazy?"

She shook her head. "I'm not saying that. But she's a mom. And for her to involve you . . ."

"Mom, it was my idea. I went to her."

She nodded. "Go ahead and help as much as you can, Ashley, but don't be surprised if this goes nowhere."

CHAPTER 56

☺ *Bryce* ☺

Mr. Cheplosa wasn't in his room when we got to school Monday morning, so Ashley and I went to our lockers, put our lunches away, then returned. His door was still locked.

Ashley told me what Mom had said, and it didn't surprise me. I'd had the same feelings but didn't want to tell her.

A few minutes before the first bell Mr. Cheplosa ran up with an armful of papers and books, fumbling for his keys while kids milled around in the hall.

Inside, Ashley pulled the photo from a big envelope.

"That will work fine," he said. "I've got to start class right now, but I'll have this done by lunch."

CHAPTER 57

✖ Ashley ✖

I hurried to Mr. Cheplosa's room just before my lunch period and found the door locked. An envelope with my name on it was taped to it. A folded sticky note read:

> Ashley,
>
> *Had to leave but here's the original and three aged photos of what she might look like at 5, 7, and 10.*

I forced myself not to peek, wanting to look at the pictures at the same time Mrs. Garcia saw them. I raced to the lunchroom and

found her busy with a bunch of kids. Bryce joined me—begging to
see the finished products (I refused)—and we ate, watching for our
chance.

Mrs. Garcia finally waved us over when there was a break in the
line. I opened the envelope and slid the photos out as we approached.
She took her plastic gloves off and wiped sweat from her forehead.

Mrs. Garcia put a hand over her mouth as we huddled, peering at
the pictures. "She's beautiful," she whispered. "How did you do
this?"

We told her. Then more kids showed up, and we had to move out
of the way. "I'll make copies of these for you," I said.

When I got home, I showed the pictures to Mom and asked if we
could go to the copy shop in town.

"Did you forget your tutoring? You're supposed to be in Memorial today."

CHAPTER 58

◎ *Bryce* ◎

I had painted the targets on the new mailbox, and it looked
great. After school I found a package inside with Sam's name on it.
He had told me to be watching for it, and I opened the box like a
hungry hyena. It was a surveillance camera you can hook up to any
TV set. I strung the cable, just enough to reach near the mailbox,
and set the camera in a bush. I plugged the other end to a black-and-
white TV we keep in an upstairs closet. The picture was clear.

Next I found an old videotape and set the VCR to record at low
speed. I turned it on and ran to the mailbox, walking up and down
the road to check the camera angle. I'm glad nobody came by because I must have looked goofy.

Back inside, I rewound the tape and laughed out loud as I moved across the screen. I needed to mount the camera higher so it would show the license plate of any vehicle coming by, so I made a platform out of some old wood and fastened it to a pine tree.

No more sleeping outside to watch for cars. I was going to have hard evidence the next time those goons drove through.

CHAPTER 59

❀ Ashley ❀

The sky had turned gray and the temperature dropped. A fog you normally see in old horror movies covered the area. It mirrored how I felt when Mom told me how much color copies of photos were likely to cost. Ouch.

Angelique met me at her school, her brown eyes wide. We went to the library and played a few games. I'll admit my mind was on other things.

Then she showed me a math homework assignment that had more red lines on it than an American flag. I went back through the paper, writing each problem again and showing her how to do it. I made up several more and turned her loose. She tried hard, but she got the wrong answer every time. I showed her again, but she didn't understand.

I saw we had gone over our time, so I stuffed my notebook in my backpack. Before I could zip it, Angelique said, "What's in that envelope?"

"Just some pictures. I have to go now—you work on these problems and we'll meet again next week."

"Pictures of what?"

"A little girl. Well, it was nice—"

"Can I see?"

It was becoming clear that math wasn't the only thing she didn't understand. I saw Mom's car, windshield wipers clicking back and forth impatiently. She hates waiting, especially if Dylan's in the car. "My mom's waiting," I said, but I knew I wasn't going to get out of here without letting her see the pictures.

She took one look at the seven-year-old version and said, "Why do you have a picture of Maria?"

"Maria?" I said, my heart fluttering. "You know her?"

"She goes to our school."

I sat down. "Are you sure?"

"It looks like her. She's Mrs. Z's daughter."

"Mrs. Z?"

"One of the kindergarten teachers," Angelique said.

"How long has she been here?"

She shrugged.

"Can you show me her room?"

Angelique took me by the hand and walked down a hall lined with essays and painted pictures.

She stopped at an open door that led to a darkened room.

Beanbag chairs were stacked against the walls, and little chairs sat around a table. At the back of the room was a desk with a date book on top and a nameplate with *Mrs. Z* written on it.

"That's Maria and her mom," Angelique said, pointing to a picture.

I gasped. The little girl, cheek to cheek with her mother and smiling, looked just like the seven-year-old version of Danielle Garcia.

CHAPTER 60

◌ *Bryce* ◌

Ashley flew out of the car and rushed into the house. "In my room. Now."

She spilled her story and showed me a black-and white photocopy of the picture of the teacher and her daughter.

"The office was open so I borrowed the photocopier. This has to be Mrs. Zoloff—don't you think?"

"You should have asked somebody at the school. Well, Mrs. Garcia should know from the picture if she can make it out."

"I can't get her hopes up by letting her see the little girl too," Ashley said. She cut the girl out of the picture and gave me the other half. "I'll be at the doctor tomorrow. Just ask Mrs. Garcia if this is Mrs. Zoloff."

"You want *me* to talk to the Lunch Lady?"

"She won't bite."

CHAPTER 61

✖ Ashley ✖

I stayed up late writing in my diary and reading. Then Mom and I
went downstairs to watch TV so I'd be good and tired for my appointment the next morning. She found an old love story with actors
I'd never heard of, and she cried at the end, but all I could think
about was the next day.

Mom turned off the TV and sat next to me, drawing a blanket
over both of us. "Whatcha thinking?"

"About Mrs. Garcia. I can't believe she's only a few miles from
her daughter."

"You don't know that this is her daughter or that Mrs. Z is even
the right person," Mom said. "Mrs. Garcia said her babysitter was
pregnant at the time. This could be Mrs. Z's real daughter."

"It has to be her."

She raised her eyebrows. "When I write a story, I think I know where I'm going to end up. But sometimes things don't turn out the way I plan. Characters take on lives of their own and go their own ways."

"This is not a book."

"It's even more important in real life to let things happen." She paused. "Like with your EEG."

"Mom, I'm scared."

She hugged me tight. We didn't say anything for a long time.

"I used to rock you to sleep when you were just a few months old," she finally whispered. "Your brother would sleep like a stone, but you had a hard time."

"Because of my seizures?"

"Could have been. We don't really know when they started. You'd go to sleep in my arms, and I'd put you in your crib. Then you'd wake up, and your dad would take over."

"I miss him," I said without looking at her.

She sighed. "So do I."

I shot her a double take. "But you have Sam."

"No one ever takes another's place. Life's kind of like a puzzle that way. When you lose someone, it's like removing a piece from your life's puzzle. That hole will always be there. But as time goes on, you add more pieces around that person, so when you stand back you can still see what the puzzle is about. The big picture. The hole is still there. It just gets smaller."

"The hole still feels big to me."

"Yeah," she said, kissing my head. "He'd be really proud of the way you care for your new family, and how you care enough about others to help try to solve their mysteries."

CHAPTER 62

◡ *Bryce* ◡

My surveillance video was still recording the next morning, but rather than watch the whole thing, I looked out and saw the mailbox still in one piece.

I wanted to get my conversation with Mrs. Garcia over with as soon as possible, but I couldn't find her before school.

At lunch, Jeff Alexander sat beside me. Jeff's been battling cancer and wears hats to hide his bald head. He was wearing the Rockies cap I had given him, which made me smile.

"I heard about your sister," Jeff said. "Bet she's scared."

"She's thinking about it all the time."

"Would it help if I talked to her?"

"She'd like that."

He promised to call later or just come over. I waited until Mrs. Garcia wasn't busy and handed her the photocopied picture of Mrs. Z.

"Recognize her?" I said.

"It's fuzzy," Mrs. Garcia said, squinting. "Who's it supposed to be?"

"You tell me."

Mrs. Garcia cocked her head. "Looks familiar. Her hair is different and her face is not clear, but it could be Tonya. I can't be sure. Where did this come from?"

Ashley had asked me not to tell. "I-I c-can't say," I said. "Ashley will talk with you tomorrow."

She stared at me.

I always figure an adult who stares at a kid without saying anything wants something. I just stared back.

CHAPTER 63

✖ Ashley ✖

The nurse hooked me up to the EEG machine and smiled. "Didn't I just see you?"

"My encore," I said.

It felt like only a few seconds passed before she woke me up, telling me the doctor would call us with the results.

I wanted to get to school and talk with Mrs. Garcia, but Mom made me go to bed. My investigation would have to wait. But as I crawled into bed I got an idea. I went to the computer, looked up a phone number, and dialed it.

"Memorial Elementary," the receptionist said.

"Yes, I'm calling about one of your kindergarten teachers. It's Mrs. Zzz . . . uh . . . how do you pronounce it?"

"Zulauf?"

It was close. "Yes, how do you spell that?"

"Z-u-l-a-u-f."

No wonder I couldn't find it. "How long has she been teaching there?"

"I think it's been two years. Are you a parent?"

"No, it's personal. I—"

"We can't give out teacher information. Good-bye."

CHAPTER 64

☻ *Bryce* ☻

After school I could hardly stand waiting for Ashley to wake up before I could tell her what Mrs. Garcia had said. While I waited, Leigh and Sam came through the living room, and she looked nervous.

Sam put a hand on my shoulder and whispered, "Gonna give it another try."

He was talking about the driver's test. There's nothing worse than trying to do something when you're really nervous. Especially when you ran into a curb the first time, and a dog almost went paws up.

Sam stopped at the front door and looked at Mom. "Did the doctor call yet?"

She shook her head and something happened between them—like each knew what the other was thinking.

Mom finally woke Ashley for dinner, and I broke the news about Mrs. Garcia.

Ashley put her head in her hands. "I feel like I'm chasing rabbits. I thought for sure she'd recognize her."

"It *was* kind of fuzzy," I said.

"Mom, when's my next tutoring day?"

"Next week. Why?"

"I'd like to go talk with Mrs. Z."

The phone rang and Mom answered. "Yes, Doctor," she said. She moved from the dinner table into the kitchen.

Ashley gritted her teeth so hard they squeaked.

Finally, Mom came back and sat down. She daintily pushed her peas around her plate and didn't look at us.

"What?!" Ashley yelled.

"What what?" Mom said.

"What did he say?" I said, just as annoyed as my sister.

"He hasn't had time to look at the results. He's been at the hospital all day. Said he'd call first thing in the morning."

"Great," Ashley said. "More rabbits."

CHAPTER 65

❀ Ashley ❀

Mom paced the living room. She pulled back the curtain and looked out the front window.

"Just call them," I said.

"No, that wouldn't be good."

"What's the worst that could happen?" I said. Mom asks me that when I'm worried. Most of the time the worst thing that could happen isn't that bad, but parroting that back to her made her scowl like a judge on one of those reality TV shows.

"Maybe she hit an elephant this time," I said.

"Not funny, Ashley."

"An aardvark?" I said. "That would be funny, wouldn't it?"

That made her smile. "Not for the aardvark," she said.

The phone rang and we raced for it. I grabbed it first. It was Derek for Bryce.

CHAPTER 66

☺ *Bryce* ☺

"Want to go to another ball game this weekend?" Derek said. "My brother's in a tournament Saturday."

"If it's okay with Leigh," I said. "She's taking her driving test now."

"Randy's gone too," Derek said. "Practice, I think. He told Mom and Dad he wouldn't be back until late."

"Really?"

"Can't wait until high school when I can stay out as late as I want even on a school night."

When I got off the phone I rewound my surveillance tape and pressed Record.

A car pulled into the driveway, and Mom rushed to the door. It was Jeff Alexander and his mom.

CHAPTER 67

Ashley

Jeff's mom talked with Mom in the kitchen while Jeff sat on the couch and pushed a Cubs cap back on his head. If it had been anybody else, I would have hated "being talked to," but I knew what Jeff had been through and that he was just trying to help.

"The hardest part of being sick is not knowing," Jeff said. "I felt bad for a long time before the doctor finally found the tumor."

"But doesn't your treatment hurt?"

"Yeah, it's a bummer to lose your hair and feel like you want to throw up all the time. But at least I know what I'm fighting. From what Bryce said, your doctor doesn't really know what to do."

"Right. But God's in control."

Jeff smiled. "But that doesn't mean everything's okay." He leaned forward. "A lot of people say that to me, and I could just scream. God has been with me through this whole thing, but I don't know how much longer I have. It may be a few years, a few months, or I could totally beat this. Do you know how that makes me feel every day?"

"Scared."

"Bingo. God even uses the times I'm scared to bring me closer to him. Just being here now to talk with you proves that. He's given me another chance to help somebody because of the stuff I've been through."

"So what would you do if you were me?"

He shrugged. "Let yourself be scared. Tell God everything you're feeling. Talk to other people too. That's helped me a lot."

Jeff's mom came back into the room and said they had to go. I hugged Jeff and thanked him.

As soon as they pulled out, Frodo's ears perked up and Pippin started growling. Mom was out of her chair and to the front door in a flash. It was neat that she cared so much for Leigh, but I have to admit that I was a little jealous.

Leigh walked in all smiles, waving a white sheet of paper.

"You didn't hit anything?" I said, then regretted it.

Leigh shrugged it off and asked Mom if she could take her to get her license tomorrow.

"We can go right after school," Mom said. "If we're not back, you'll be okay, won't you, Ashley?"

"Me and the other latchkey kid will be fine," I said.

"Thanks, Dad," Leigh said. She hugged him and skipped up the stairs.

Dylan came out of Bryce's room, and Leigh picked him up and

twirled him around. "I passed my driver's test!" she shouted. "I have to call Randy!"

"He's not home," Bryce said. "I talked with Derek a few minutes ago. Randy's at softball practice and won't be back until late."

Bryce glanced at me, and I knew we were both thinking the same thing.

CHAPTER 68

◑ *Bryce* ◑

The next morning I hit the Rewind button on my surveillance tape and went downstairs to grab a bowl of cereal. When I got back, I turned on the monitor. The picture showed the camera was lying in the grass on its side. A tree blocked the view of the mailbox.

I slammed my cereal bowl down. I wanted to scream, but Dylan was still asleep.

I pushed the Play button and saw the whole video was shot from the grass. I ran outside and inspected the line running from the house to the camera. It looked as if someone had tripped over it, which would have yanked the camera to the ground. Dylan had been running outside the evening before. Maybe I couldn't blame Randy for this.

It was getting close to school time, so I pushed Play, then held down the Fast Forward button. Everything was black, but I noticed a blip on the screen at about midnight and returned to normal speed.

The sound was muffled, but I heard a vehicle pass, turn around, and come back. I bet it was Randy's truck.

Then it happened. Someone whooped, then a whack, and a guy yelped and cursed. The voice sounded familiar. Was it Randy? I'd certainly never heard him use those words before.

Then the truck peeled out and raced away. My camera would have been in perfect position to capture the license plate—if it hadn't been on the ground.

I got dressed and came down to find Ashley eating breakfast.

"They came back last night," I said.

"Great! You got them on tape?"

I shook my head. "Dylan must have knocked it off. I got them swearing when they hit the box, but you can't see anything."

I hurried out to the mailbox where I noticed a dent in one side. I couldn't imagine what it must have felt like to hit concrete with a bat.

On the ground lay a splinter of wood with blotchy lettering on the side. So Randy had graduated from aluminum to wood.

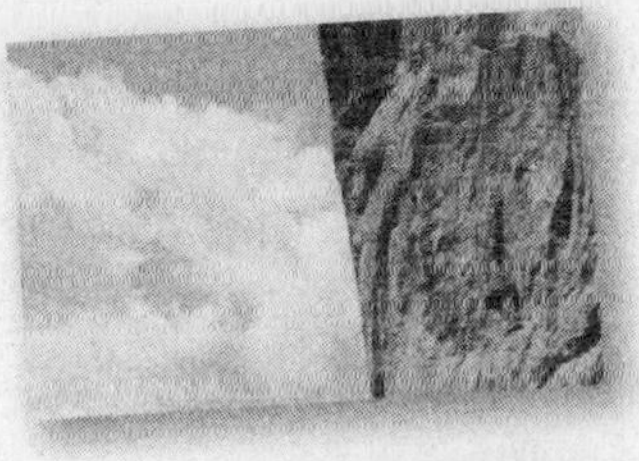

CHAPTER 69

❀ Ashley ❀

The doctor still hadn't called by the time Bryce and I left for school. I told Mom I'd call her at lunch to find out what he said.

As if enough wasn't going on in my life, I had a test in Ancient Civilizations and got the Mayans and the Romans mixed up.

At lunch Mrs. Garcia thanked me for what I was doing. "It's enough that someone believes me. I never thought anyone would."

"If you're right, we're going to find Danielle," I said. "Is there any chance your babysitter's name was Zulauf and not Zoloff?"

She shrugged. "I'm not too good with names."

Bryce came up as I walked to the phone. "I just heard some mailboxes near town were smashed last night."

"Really?"

He nodded. "Talk to Mom yet?"

I shook my head.

"Use my cell," he said.

I dialed and my hands shook.

"I'm worried about Leigh," Bryce said. "If she knew her boyfriend was—"

I raised a hand as Mom picked up the phone. I just wanted the facts. (Actually, I didn't want to hear anything but that the doctor couldn't find anything wrong with me.)

"Bottom line," Mom said, "the doctor still doesn't like what he sees. He's considering other options. Another change of medicine. Blood tests. That kind of thing."

I didn't want to cry, but I couldn't help it. Bryce, who didn't usually do this kind of thing, put an arm around me.

"I hate this," I whispered. "I wouldn't wish this on Boo Heckler."

"Might be an improvement for him," Bryce said, and I had to smile.

My biggest fear was that I would never grow out of this. Jeff's words came back to me as I whispered a prayer.

CHAPTER 70

☺ *Bryce* ☺

Leigh showed off her license that evening, though the picture looked like one of those wanted criminals you see on TV. "Can I drive over and show Randy?"

Mom said she could, and Leigh bounded up the stairs to get ready.

I cornered Mom. "You sure you want to let her go to his house?"

"It's not that far, Bryce."

"I don't mean the driving. . . ." I hadn't told Mom what I suspected, so I caught Leigh as she headed out the door.

"You might not want to spend so much time with Randy," I said. She slowed and glared at me. "Why?"

I followed her onto the porch. "He might be mixed up in something bad."

"Like what?"

"I can't say."

"You don't know what you're talking about."

"How could you know if I know what I'm talking about if you don't even know what I'm talking about?"

She stared at me. "What?"

"I have proof," I said, but she jumped in the car and drove away.

CHAPTER 71

✵ Ashley ✵

To take my mind off the doctor's report, I sat at the computer and tried to find a phone number for Mrs. Zulauf. I came up empty, so I found a site that would find anyone's number in the U.S. for only $9.95. It would also tell if the person had a criminal record, a traffic ticket, even what that person's neighborhood was like.

I asked Mom if I could use her credit card, and she frowned. "Do you have 10 dollars?"

I checked my wallet. Two dollars. "I'll babysit Dylan for the rest of it."

Mom gave me a knowing look and sat at the computer. "Sam and

I can go out to dinner this weekend." She entered her credit card information and clicked the mouse. "Okay, you're set. But this gives you only one search."

I typed in all the information I knew and clicked the Search button.

The computer whirred and acted like it was choking. Then the screen turned blue, and a green light at the bottom pulsed *searching*. My heart pounded with each flash as I hoped, prayed.

Finally a window popped up, and the following appeared on the screen:

Tonya Zulauf
2342 Shore Lane
Memorial, CO

It also showed her unlisted phone number and listed her daughter's name as Maria. I nearly knocked Mom over when I stood.

"Sorry," she said. "Just looking."

CHAPTER 72

◎ *Bryce* ◎

I followed Sam to the barn. When he put his cell phone away, he said he'd been talking to a Colorado Rockies baseball player, who had recently been taken off the disabled list. "He just got the okay from his doctor to join the team in San Diego. Wants to know if I can get him there for the game tonight."

"Can you?"

"Gonna try. What's up?"

"It can wait."

Sam sat on the edge of his desk. "Come on. I've got time."

I traced a line on his carpet with my shoe. "What if you think you know someone who did something wrong, but you're afraid of getting that person in trouble because . . ."

"Because?"

". . . that person is a friend of someone related to you? And that person could be locked up for a long time."

Sam scratched at his mustache. "How sure are you?"

"All the clues point to one person."

"Randy."

I nodded, wondering how he knew.

"How much evidence?"

I laid out everything.

Sam folded his arms. "That is a lot, but it's all circumstantial. Know what that means?"

I took a stab. "It's not enough?"

"It means you have a lot of reasons but nothing concrete."

"There's concrete in the mailbox."

Sam smiled. "Pun unintended. Anyway, don't jump to conclusions when you're not 100 percent sure."

I didn't like Sam's answer, but I knew he was right. "What if I want to warn this person that he's being watched?"

Sam chewed the inside of his cheek. "I suppose if it were me I'd appreciate it. And if I were that person's girlfriend, I'd appreciate it even more."

CHAPTER 73

✿ Ashley ✿

I dialed the number but nearly hung up before the answering machine picked up.

"Hi, it's Tonya and Maria. Leave a message and we'll call you back."

"Here comes the beep!" Maria said.

I hung up before the beep. Mrs. Z was the only mother Maria had ever known. Maybe she really *was* Mrs. Z's child. Could Mrs. Garcia be using me?

Later Bryce and I watched a show about the police reopening an old case to figure out a murder. To find out the identity of a body, they took a strand of hair and did DNA testing on it. With that they were able to tell who the dead person was related to.

If I could get strands of hair from Maria and from Mrs. Garcia and have them analyzed, we could find out for sure if they were mother and daughter.

☺ *Bryce* ☺

Ashley's strong-minded and has her own way of doing things, but I could tell the doctor stuff was wearing her down. At lunch two days later I thought she'd flipped her lid when she asked to borrow one of my sandwich bags for Mrs. Garcia's hair.

"The bag has peanut butter in it."

"I don't care."

Mrs. Garcia didn't seem half as mean as she used to. Ashley whispered to her, and while Mrs. Garcia gave her a strange look, she took off her plastic gloves and pulled out a couple of strands of hair.

Ashley stuffed them into the peanut-butter bag and headed for her next class.

"Now all I need is a DNA expert," Ashley said. "And one more thing."

CHAPTER 75

❀ Ashley ❀

I rushed home after school to run errands with Mom. I asked her to drop me off at the elementary school just before it let out so I could give Angelique something. But of course that wasn't my only reason.

I went by Angelique's room and peeked in. I thought about interrupting, but I waited until the bell rang to get her attention. She ran over to me, and I gave her a bag of goodies. "Hope you like them."

"Thanks!" she said, beaming.

"Do you think you could help me find Maria?"

"Mrs. Z's daughter?" she said. "Sure. There she is."

The sight took my breath away. Mr. Cheplosa's picture had come to life. Her teeth were a little shorter, and her hair a little longer, but her face was so close it was amazing.

She looked at me suspiciously as I held out my hand. "Hi, I'm Ashley, Angelique's tutor."

"Hi," she said, grabbing her backpack. I noticed a hair on her shoulder. I brushed at it, then picked it off.

"Excuse me?" a woman said from behind me.

I jumped and turned around.

"Hi, Mrs. Z!" Angelique said.

"Hello," the woman said, not taking her eyes off me.

I dropped the hair and reached out to shake her hand. She shook like she had a dead fish at the end of her arm.

"I'm Ashley, Mrs. Z," I said, smiling and pumping the fish up and down. "Angelique told me about your daughter."

She squinted. "Do you have a reason to be here during school?"

"Just dropping off a present to the best . . . tutee in school. She's really making progress—"

Mrs. Z turned on her heel and walked Maria down the hall. The girl looked back as they rounded the corner.

I looked at the floor, but the strand of hair had disappeared.

CHAPTER 76

☺ *Bryce* ☺

On Saturday Randy's team would play two games—
assuming they won the first—so Derek and I had plenty of time to
explore the nearby park.

I bought a big bag of red licorice when we got there, and within
an hour I had finished the whole thing. My stomach felt like it was
going to explode, so I wound up stretching out in the backseat of
Randy's truck. I left the windows down, hoping for a cool breeze.

"Randy, lover boy, get over here!" someone yelled.

"Here he comes," someone else said. "The Red Rock Casanova."

The first game must have been over. They were laughing and

sounding happy, so they must have won. It sounded like half a dozen guys. I wondered if Leigh was with them. Didn't sound like it.

"We're watching the final tape tonight, Randy," a younger voice said. "Did you make a copy of it?"

"It's in my glove compartment," Randy said.

"How about we watch it at your house?"

"I don't know," Randy said. "My brother's a pest, and my mom and dad are home."

"We can go to my house," another said.

I felt even worse, and it wasn't from the licorice. I scrunched back as far as I could and hoped they couldn't see me.

CHAPTER 77

❀ Ashley ❀

I stood behind Mom and looked into the mirror as she put on her earrings. She was wearing a dress too. She and Sam were about to take me up on my babysitting debt. Dylan was pumped that we were going to eat pizza and watch a movie.

"Mom, remember that guy you interviewed for the murder mystery you wrote?"

She paused. "The DNA expert in St. Louis? Sure. Officer Jim Deavers."

"Do you know if he liked the book?"

"Matter of fact, he did. I gave him credit in the front and sent him copies to pass around."

"How long does it take to analyze DNA?"

Mom turned so fast I thought she was going to smear her lipstick. "Why? What are you up to?"

"Just investigating," I said, retreating a step.

"Ashley, you have to be really careful with things like this. You're not looking for a lost coin or who ate the last Twinkie. These are people's lives. They have a right to their privacy."

"But if Mrs. Garcia's daughter is who I think she is, doesn't she have rights too?"

Mom pursed her lips and sighed. "When you get older, you'll understand that Mrs. Garcia is a troubled woman. I've learned some things about her."

"Like what?"

Mom sat on the bed and ran her hand across the spread. "She's . . . she's . . . well, a little unpredictable. People aren't sure if the things she says are always true. And you said yourself that she's been in three different schools—"

"She's been looking for her daughter." I was insulted that Mom thought I could be fooled. But what if Mrs. Garcia *wasn't* telling the truth? What if *she* was the one who wanted to steal a child? Maybe she was using me?

Sam knocked. He was wearing cowboy boots, a Western shirt, new jeans, and a hat the size of Oklahoma. "You look nice, hon," he said. He looked at me. "Dylan's counting the minutes."

Mom put a hand on my shoulder and kissed my forehead. "Don't forget to take your medicine tonight."

Adults!

CHAPTER 78

☺ *Bryce* ☺

I stayed as still as I could and prayed the guys would leave. It was clear there was a bunch of them involved, and I wondered how the police would charge all of them. Their voices trailed off, so I thought I was in the clear.

Then the door opened. It was Derek. "How are you feeling?"

"Like I never want to see another piece of licorice in my life."

"Wanna watch the second game? It's for the championship."

"Give me a few more minutes," I said.

When Derek left, I sat up. My stomach churned and my head spun. I had to get out of the truck.

I didn't want a repeat of a year before. At a carnival I had eaten two corn dogs slathered in mustard, then played miniature golf. Then Ashley pointed to the Tilt-A-Whirl and said she would race me. She barely beat me. We were three spins in when I remembered the corn dogs. Or, I should say, they remembered me. Let's just say it wasn't pretty.

I climbed out of the truck and took a deep breath. From the diamond I could hear them announcing the starting lineups.

I moved to the front of the truck, slid in the passenger side, and popped open the glove compartment. Underneath a pile of napkins was a videotape. The same tape I had seen under Randy's bed—the one with the smudged word *mailbox* on it.

"What're you doing?"

I nearly lost my licorice. It was Leigh.

"Getting ready to come to the game," I said.

"Derek said you weren't feeling well."

"I'm okay now," I said. But I wasn't. In fact I felt even sicker about the whole thing.

Like Sam said, every clue before this had been "circumstantial." I finally had the "concrete" I'd been looking for.

CHAPTER 79

✖ Ashley ✖

I doodled in the sandbox beside Dylan while our pizza cooked. All I could think of was Mrs. Garcia and Danielle. For all I knew, she had stolen a picture of Mrs. Z's baby. No wonder the girl looked like the computer-generated older picture.

I told Dylan I'd be right back and went in to check the pizza time. Still a few minutes to go. In the kitchen I found Mom's day planner. I turned to her work section and looked up the phone number for Jim Deavers in St. Louis. I took the cordless phone outside so I could be with Dylan.

It took a while for Officer Deavers to come to the phone, and I apologized for bothering him at home. When he found out who I was he laughed and said it wasn't a problem.

"I'm working on a missing person case," I said, then felt dumb for calling it a case. I asked how long it would take to analyze hair from two different people to see if they're related.

"The technology is improving all the time. Probably a few days."

I took a breath. "If I sent the samples, could you look at them?"

"Not a problem," Mr. Deavers said. "As long as your mom makes me famous in one of her next books." The phone clicked, and he said he was getting another call.

I held on for a few minutes, then hung up. I figured I would talk with him in a few days.

Dylan pointed at the house. "Ashley, what's that noise?"

CHAPTER 80

○ *Bryce* ○

Randy had a single in the first inning, a double in the third, and a homer with one out in the bottom of the seventh to give his team the championship. Who knows, maybe he would have hit a triple and hit for the cycle if he'd had another turn at bat. The players walked off the field sweaty and dirty, looking like they needed a garden hose.

Leigh gave Randy a big hug, even though he was filthy, and I felt worse for her all the time. She had to know the truth—and soon.

"Bryce," Randy said, "could you carry this to the back of the truck?" He handed me his trophy and a long, heavy, green duffel bag.

Derek helped. It was a bear trying to lug the thing over the side of the pickup into the back. When we did, the top of the bag opened and a few bats and balls fell out.

I hopped in and was shoving them back in when I noticed a wood bat among all the metal ones. I turned it over. A big piece was missing on the front, right around the Louisville Slugger imprint.

I made sure the other stuff was put away and jumped down. "Randy, could I take this bat home to practice?"

Leigh raised an eyebrow. "We have bats at home—"

"It's okay," Randy said. "Just remember where you got it."

How can I forget?

CHAPTER 81

❈ Ashley ❈

I rushed into the kitchen, where the smoke alarm was screeching, and the smell and smoke overwhelmed me.

I turned the oven off, then found some mitts and opened the door. I had hit Broil instead of Bake. Our pizza had turned into a hockey puck. Not an inch was edible. I dropped it into the sink and turned on the water, making it hiss and smoke even more.

Dylan was scared and stood there crying. I held him and he buried his face in my shoulder. "I want my ba-ba."

His ba-ba is his favorite cup with a screw-on lid. I sat him at the table and looked in the cabinets, in his room, outside, everywhere. It wasn't until I moved the black mess in the sink that I found it. Dylan's ba-ba was stuck to the bottom of the pizza pan, melted.

"How about if we let you drink from a big-boy cup tonight?"

"No, I want my ba-ba."

"I can make you lemonade," I said.

He snorted and big tears ran down his cheeks. That always happens when he's tired. Finally he nodded, and I quickly made the lemonade before he changed his mind.

I opened the windows in the kitchen and living room, so the air would push the smoke out. The wind had picked up and was blowing a mist toward us from the mountains. It looked spooky.

The smoke detector finally stopped blaring. I was trying to figure out what we could eat when the phone rang. The caller ID showed the number unavailable, and when I picked up nobody was there.

I put a peanut-butter-and-jelly sandwich and some chips in front of Dylan and made myself a sandwich too. I reached in the cupboard for my medicine. I shook the bottles and the pills rattled. *What good are these things doing me?*

The phone rang, and caller ID read unavailable again.

"Hello, this is Ashley."

There was silence, but whoever it was didn't hang up.

"Hello?" I said.

"You were at the school the other day," a woman said. "Memorial Elementary."

"Yes, I was."

"Stay away from my daughter."

CHAPTER 02

◎ *Bryce* ◎

At home later, I raced for the hidden splinter. Like a puzzle piece, it fit the bat perfectly. That's what I call concrete. I didn't even need the videotape, which was still in Randy's glove compartment.

I ran inside to tell Ashley and smelled smoke. I thought she'd had another seizure, her face was so pale. She told me about what had happened with the pizza and the phone call from Mrs. Z.

"You've gotten under her skin, Ash," I said. "She must have something to hide."

I told Ashley what I'd heard at the softball game and about the final clue.

"What are you going to do?" she said.

"We should give Randy a chance to confess before we go to the police," I said. "Shouldn't we?"

"Yeah, but what if he gets mad?"

I hadn't thought of that. Would Randy do something to me if I told him I knew the truth?

CHAPTER 83

Ashley

Mom and Sam looked happy when they came back from dinner until they discovered what had happened. The smoke alarm was nothing compared to the phone call.

"I'm just glad it was only smoke," Mom said. "Now what did this woman say again?"

When I repeated it, Sam's face twisted and he looked mad. The phone rang and he answered it. He covered the mouthpiece. "Ashley, did you talk with an Officer Deavers tonight?"

"Yeah, why?"

"He's asking when you can have samples to him."

I just stared at Sam and tried to look innocent. He told Deavers we would get back to him and hung up.

"Did you try to get something from that little girl for Jim to analyze?" Sam said.

I nodded. "A hair."

"No wonder her mother is so upset," Mom said.

"I didn't even keep it. It fell on the floor."

"How did she get our number?" Mom said.

I shrugged. "Maybe she has caller ID . . ."

"So you called her first?"

"Yeah, that was the number I paid to get."

Mom looked frustrated, but Sam looked like he was fighting a smile—like I was doing something Mom would do, investigate, get to the bottom of things.

"Ashley," Mom said, "you simply can't—"

Sam put an arm around her. "Let's sleep on this," he said.

CHAPTER 84

◎ *Bryce* ◎

All I could think about the next morning in Sunday school was how to talk with Randy and what he might do to me. If I could talk him into going to the police and confessing, maybe they'd go easy on him. Maybe if he paid for all the repairs he could get out of going to jail. Then again, he could bonk me on the head, jump in his truck, and head for Mexico.

Apparently I missed my teacher asking me a question. Everybody laughed when I looked up suddenly and said, "Huh?"

"Good answer, Timberline," Duncan said.

At lunch I asked Sam if he would take me to Randy's house later.

"You sure?"

I nodded. "Just give me a few minutes at the computer to write down all the evidence."

I printed the document and found Sam in the living room reading the paper. "I'm ready," I said.

"Good," he said, "because Randy just pulled up."

Maybe I wasn't ready after all. Afraid of losing my nerve, I rushed out and intercepted Randy before he got to the door. "Do you have a minute?" I said.

"Sure. What's up?"

My stomach suddenly felt like a thousand licorice sticks had snuck inside and were squirming for the best position. "I-I . . . I think we should go back to your truck."

"Okay," Randy said slowly.

As we walked back, I scanned my list of clues.

He stopped, folded his arms, and leaned against the truck.

I took a deep breath. "I know about the mailbox bashing, and I know you were involved."

Randy's eyebrows went up. "Me?"

"Yeah, and if you turn yourself in you might not have to go to jail."

Randy narrowed his eyes at me. "You're kidding, right?"

I read from my list. "Your bat has the same color paint on it as our old mailbox. At your house I found a videotape with *mailbox* written on it. The bashers drove a truck that sounds like yours. You were out late with your friends the same night a bunch of mailboxes got creamed. You also had fireworks in your truck. The police talked to you at the video store. At the game last night I overheard your friends tell you they were going to watch the tape you had in your glove compartment—the same tape I saw at your house."

Randy put his fingers through his belt loops. "Is that all?"

"No. The other night somebody tried to bash our mailbox again—only this time they used a wood bat. A splinter came off and I kept it. It matches the bat you let me borrow."

That seemed to hit Randy hard. He ran a hand through his hair and sucked in a breath. "You done?"

"Yeah."

"Can I have the bat?" Randy said.

"Um, no. Not yet. It's evidence."

He shook his head. "You think I would do that to my girlfriend's mailbox? You think I'm the kind of person who enjoys trashing other people's property?"

"Maybe it was peer pressure. They say it's bad in high school. Maybe you never swung the bat, but if you drove—"

"I didn't do it," Randy said, his teeth clenched. "The police talked to me about my front license plate. It's bent up and unreadable. I *was* out with the guys several times, but we never did anything wrong."

"What about the video?" I said.

Randy went to his glove compartment and handed me the tape. "This one?"

"Yeah, it says *Mailbox.*"

"It says *Matrix,*" Randy said. "The label got smudged."

It felt like he had punched me in the stomach. Finally, I said, "So you were watching this with your friends last night?"

"We watched a funny highlight tape of our season. One of the guys dubbed all our muffed plays and strikeouts onto this. Here, take it. See for yourself."

"What about the night you said an emergency—?"

"One of the guys hurt his arm," Randy said. "Turned out to be broken. We drove him to the hospital."

Sam's words came back to me about jumping to conclusions.

"What about the bats?" I said. "The one with the paint on it?"

"The paint could have come from the fence around the ball field. Some of the guys throw their bats against it and the paint rubs off."

I can't believe it. He has an answer for everything. "And the splintered one?"

"That's a problem," Randy said.

"Then you're guilty?"

Randy shook his head. "It's not my bat. I don't actually know whose it is. They all got mixed up with each other at practice."

I felt like a jerk and tried to cover. "Then if we find out whose bat this is, we'll find the basher?"

Leigh ran toward us. "I didn't know you were here."

"Just having a powwow with your brother."

"Anything wrong?" Leigh said.

"Nothing we can't handle," Randy said.

Leigh got in the truck and I just stood there, like my feet were planted in the gravel. "I'm really sorry," I said, my voice shaky. "I—"

Randy put a hand on my shoulder. "Listen. All those clues. I would have thought the same thing."

"But it's probably one of your friends, isn't it?"

He frowned. "'Fraid so. Give the video a look. It's pretty funny."

CHAPTER 85

✖ Ashley ✖

Monday morning Mrs. Garcia ran to Bryce and me outside the school. "Any news?"

I nodded. "I saw the girl who might be your daughter Friday. I tried to—"

"Where?" Mrs. Garcia said. "I have to see her."

"But—but I-I—"

Bryce stepped forward. "Her mother warned Ashley to stay away."

Mrs. Garcia's eyes flashed. "She doesn't want you to find my baby."

"If this is your daughter," I said, "she's not a baby anymore."

"I know that. Nothing will keep me from finding her. Tell me where you saw her."

I couldn't—not yet. I didn't know who to believe anymore. "We have to go," I said.

"Tell me where she is, Ashley," Mrs. Garcia said. She stood in our way, hands on her hips.

"Hi, Mr. Forster!" Bryce yelled.

That was enough to get Mrs. Garcia to turn, and in that split second we were past her and into the crowd inside the school.

CHAPTER 86

○ *Bryce* ○

I didn't go near the cafeteria, and Ashley met me outside for lunch. We planned how we would split up if Mrs. Garcia came out.

Derek saw us and walked over. I was afraid Randy had told him about my accusation, but Derek didn't mention it.

"Randy wants you to come over tonight. Six o'clock."

"What for?" I said.

"A team picnic. Guys coming to get their equipment. Said you might want to be there."

When Derek left, Ashley said, "Be careful. Randy could be setting you up."

"What do you mean?"

"What if he was lying and is going to make you pay for nosing around?"

"Ash, I watched the video. It's not about mailboxes. It's softballs banging off people's legs, guys with big guts tripping over first base, that kind of stuff."

"You still should be careful."

Jeff Alexander saw us and waved. "How's the new medicine?"

"I can't tell much difference," Ashley said. "Thanks for asking."

He turned to me. "I talked with my dad about the bike trip this summer." Jeff had a dream of riding in a benefit bike trip that raised money for cancer research. There was no way he could do it himself and his father had a bad back or something, so Jeff asked me to go with him on a tandem bike. "All we have to do is raise the money and we're there."

He held out his hand and I slapped it. "I'm with you."

Ashley grabbed my arm and nodded toward the back door of the school. Mrs. Garcia had stepped out and was looking around. We scooted past Jeff and slipped inside before she saw us.

CHAPTER 87

✖ Ashley ✖

The last thing I wanted to do was tutor in Memorial that night, but Mom wouldn't let me out of it.

"But what if I see Mrs. Z?"

She pressed her lips together. "I'll be in the car in the parking lot. If anything happens, call me."

"Let's work in the library today, Angelique," I said. "It's more cozy."

We played a game of Sorry, and before we started on her homework, Angelique went to the bathroom.

I sensed someone behind me and turned to see a young face with doe eyes, soft and pretty. Maria—or was it Danielle?

"You're Ashley, the one my mom called."

"Yeah, but—"

"Why did you take that hair from me?"

No way could I tell her the whole story. "I'm an amateur detective," I said. "I just want to look at your hair and see what it says about you."

"What it says about me?"

I nodded, searching for words. "Our bodies have codes that tell who we're related to, things like that."

"Really? Can it tell me who my daddy is?"

"Maybe. Don't you know?"

She shook her head. "My mom won't tell me. Except he's one of the bad people."

"The bad people?"

Maria nodded. "Bad people try to get me. My mom thinks you're one of them. But Angelique says you're the nicest."

"I'm not trying to get you. I'm just—"

"Mom said if the bad people find us, we'll have to move. She keeps saying it was a mistake to come here, that we should have gone far away. Sometimes I think *she's* the bad people."

What was I supposed to say to that? "Why?"

"She's mean to me, yells at me, hits me sometimes. If I make a friend, she'll say they're bad and that I can't play with them anymore. She won't tell me why I don't have a dad. But I have to have one, don't I?"

My mind was reeling. "What if I told you your daddy might have been a soldier?"

"That would be neat. Is it true?"

"I don't know. Maybe."

She thought for a moment, then plucked out one of her own strands of hair and handed it to me. Someone called her name, and she hurried out of the library.

CHAPTER 88

◡ *Bryce* ◡

I helped Ashley put the hair samples carefully in clear plastic bags, and Sam let us use his overnight shipping account to send them to St. Louis. The FedEx truck pulled into the driveway before 5:00, and the driver picked up the package.

"Maria won't say anything to her mother about giving you the hair, will she?"

"I hope not," Ashley said. "But she's awfully young."

I rode with Leigh to Randy's. She thought I was just going there to play with Derek. He met us out front, and we shot baskets in his backyard for a while.

Finally, Randy called us in and pulled me aside. "Let's see who takes the wood bat. Then you can call the police." He was as interested in this as I was, which made me feel even worse about having accused him.

His teammates started arriving a few minutes later, and Randy fired up the grill. He had a cooler filled with sodas and more hamburgers than I'd ever seen stacked up beside it. Somebody brought out a TV and turned on the Rockies game. A few guys went into the field behind Randy's house and shagged fly balls, while others sat talking or played horseshoes.

I was glad when it was time for everybody to go home because I wanted the mystery solved. Randy's coach stood on a picnic table and gave out awards for most pulled muscles, most bruises, most valuable "prayer" (for the one with the lowest batting average), that kind of thing.

Then he talked about how he had let the team down for being such a poor representative of Jesus. "Frankly, I'm sorry for the way I acted a lot of the time. I wish I could go back and change things. One thing's for sure: I'm workin' on it and will do better next year, with the Lord's help. A lot of you don't come to church that often, and when you do, it's only to qualify for the team."

Some of the guys chuckled nervously.

"But church is not just some place to go on Sundays. It can be exciting, an adventure." The coach pulled out a New Testament and read a few verses about how God loves everyone and sent Jesus to die for our sins. It was neat how everybody got real quiet and listened. In the end, he asked everybody to consider coming to church regularly to find out what a relationship with God was all about. It was probably the best sermon I'd heard that wasn't a sermon.

"Congratulations on the championship," the coach said, "and I'd love to have all of you back next season."

Randy thanked everyone for coming and told them to take some more soda and burgers before they left. "And don't forget to pick up your stray equipment."

Guys crowded around the picnic table and picked up hats and gloves and bats. The wood one just lay there until a skinny guy with a fresh cast on his arm sauntered up and grabbed it.

I had to wonder if he'd broken his arm smacking our concrete mailbox. "Who's that?" I whispered.

Randy told me, but I didn't recognize the name.

As the guy took another cheeseburger I said, "Nice bat. How'd you get that notch in it?"

"It's not mine. I'm picking it up for my cousin. He left it at practice last week."

"He plays on the team?"

He turned and eyed me. "Been trying to get him to, but he won't come to church. Plus, he's a little young, 'bout your age probably. Name's Aaron. Aaron Heckler. You might know him. Everybody calls him Boo."

It shouldn't have surprised me that Boo Heckler had been involved, especially with *our* mailbox, but there was no way he had driven the truck—he must have had help.

Sam drove me to the police station after school the next day, and I talked with one of the officers I had worked with before. He took notes, and I could tell by the way he lifted his eyebrows now and then that he was impressed.

"You've got quite a detective here, Mr. Timberline," he told Sam. "We still have to find out who was in on this with Heckler, so we'll confront him with the evidence and see what he says."

"Does he have to know I turned him in?" I said.

"I won't tell him if you won't," the officer said, winking.

CHAPTER 89

✖ Ashley ✖

One day turned into two, then three, and when we reached the weekend I gave up hope of ever hearing from the DNA guy. But on Monday when I got home from school Mom told me, "Mr. Deavers called. Wants you to call him right away."

I held my breath and my fingers shook when I dialed. Waiting for him to answer was like waiting for Christmas, but he finally picked up.

"I suppose you'd like to know what I found," he said.

Why do adults always do that? "I can't wait!"

"Well, I'm not sure why there was peanut butter all over one strand, but the two hair samples you sent match genetically."

"What does that mean?"

He laughed. "It means they come from blood relatives. These two are mother and daughter."

I screamed, jumped up and down, thanked Mr. Deavers, and hugged Mom. Christmas had finally come.

Mr. Deavers said he would send the results overnight. I went to tell Bryce, but he was still at the police department. Mom was just as excited as I was, and we hugged each other and danced around the kitchen. I was about to call Mrs. Garcia, but Mom pointed at the clock. "Tutor time. Anyway, this is something you need to tell her in person."

I was still afraid of Mrs. Z, but I had to walk into that school. I guessed I'd know soon enough if Maria/Danielle had told her "mother" about the hair sample. Neither was in sight when I got there.

I found Angelique, but I could barely think, let alone concentrate on her work. She showed me the page I had given her the last time we'd met, and to my surprise, she'd gotten almost all of them right. But she didn't seem very excited when I told her she was improving.

"What's wrong?" I said.

Her little lip turned up. "Bad news. Mrs. Z and Maria are gone."

"What do you mean?"

"She quit and they moved away."

I ran to the office and found the receptionist. "Is it true?" I said. "Mrs. Z is gone?"

She scowled. "Yes. She gave notice Friday. Really put us in a bind."

"Do you know where she went?"

She shook her head. "I think she has relatives in Arizona, but I'm not sure. It's sad. The kids are devastated." She cocked her head. "You're not Ashley, are you?"

I nodded, and she pulled out an envelope with my name scrawled on the front. "Maria came to me Friday with tears streaming. She said she didn't know your last name but that you came to tutor a couple of times a week."

I thanked the woman, said good-bye to Angelique, and headed outside to be alone. I sat on a stone bench, waiting for Mom and staring at the envelope. I couldn't believe I had gone from being so happy to so sad in one afternoon.

I opened it and pulled out a lined piece of paper, the kind they teach you how to write on in second grade. The handwriting was small and took up only a few lines.

> *Dear Ashly,*
>
> *Mom says we have to go away. The bad people are coming. I dont know where we going. I wish I could talk to you again. Your nice.*
>
> *Love,*
> *Maria*

I put my head in my hands and cried.

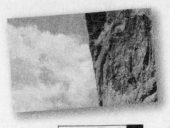

CHAPTER 90

☺ *Bryce* ☺

It was pretty cool of Randy to not hold it against me that I had suspected him. I was afraid he and Leigh would both stop talking to me, but Randy treated me the same as before, and as far as I know, he didn't even tell Leigh. Or maybe he did and she didn't make a big deal of it.

Not long after that the phone rang, and Sam handed it to me. It was the same officer I had talked with. He said they had gone out to Boo's house, but he swore he didn't know anything about the mailboxes.

"When we pulled out the bat you gave us, he went white as a

sheet," the officer said. "He finally broke down and confessed that he had done some of the bashing and that someone had given him fireworks that he used in Mrs. Watson's mailbox and some others on her street."

"But he couldn't have done all that alone," I said.

"Right. He gave us two names of some older guys. They're in some trouble."

"What will happen to Boo?"

"We're trying to work out something with his parents. He might actually have to go to the detention center."

I felt bad for Boo. The detention center housed kids who were 10 times meaner than him. I hoped he wouldn't find out who had turned him in.

It felt good to know the truth, finally, but not as good as when Ashley handed the DNA results to Mrs. Garcia. The woman burst into tears and had to sit down. Mom and Sam told her they'd do anything they could to help her find her little girl.

When Mrs. Garcia finished looking at the letter from the DNA guy, she grabbed Ashley and hugged her. Then she hugged me. If you would have told me two weeks before that the Lunch Lady would be hugging anybody in our school, I would have said you were crazy.

EPILOGUE

❀ Ashley ❀

A month later the phone rang while Bryce and I were trying to finish the waterfall puzzle. We were talking about how we dreaded having to go back to school in the fall, though we both thought eighth grade would be kind of cool.

Mom answered and talked for a while, though she kept looking at me. Finally she hung up. "They found Maria," she said. "Mrs. Z applied at a school in Wyoming, and the authorities tracked her down. Mrs. Garcia is going there to meet her daughter for the first time today."

The next day *The Gazette* from Colorado Springs ran a long story about the reunion, and it was all over the network news too. Mrs. Z was in jail, and Danielle was returned to her real mother. Tonya confessed to taking the child after she learned she couldn't have children of her own. She had lied about being pregnant, then had taken Mrs. Garcia's baby and started the fire to cover up the crime.

The paper didn't explain how Mrs. Garcia had found her little girl, and that was okay. It was enough for me to see the picture of them together, hugging and smiling and crying.

Dr. Alek changed my medicine one more time and said we'd have to keep working on it. I guess you just have to live with some things, and with Jeff's help I saw that God could be drawing me closer to himself through all the bad stuff going on in my life.

Bryce and I finished the waterfall puzzle after working on it for weeks, with help from Sam, Leigh, and Mom. We put our last piece in on a Sunday morning before church and realized there was still one missing.

Dylan ran through the room giggling, and later we found out why. When Mom changed his Spider-Man underwear, she found the last piece in there.

Finally a puzzle that won't have to live with a missing piece.

About the Authors

Jerry B. Jenkins (jerryjenkins.com) is the writer of the Left Behind series. He owns the Jerry B. Jenkins Christian Writers Guild, an organization dedicated to mentoring aspiring authors. Former vice president for publishing for the Moody Bible Institute of Chicago, he also served many years as editor of *Moody* magazine and is now Moody's writer-at-large.

His writing has appeared in publications as varied as *Reader's Digest, Parade, Guideposts,* in-flight magazines, and dozens of other periodicals. Jenkins's biographies include books with Billy Graham, Hank Aaron, Bill Gaither, Luis Palau, Walter Payton, Orel Hershiser, and Nolan Ryan, among many others. His books appear regularly on the *New York Times, USA Today, Wall Street Journal,* and *Publishers Weekly* best-seller lists.

Jerry is also the writer of the nationally syndicated sports story comic strip *Gil Thorp,* distributed to newspapers across the United States by Tribune Media Services.

Jerry and his wife, Dianna, live in Colorado and have three grown sons and three grandchildren.

Chris Fabry is a writer and broadcaster who lives in Colorado. He has written more than 40 books, including collaboration on the Left Behind: The Kids series.

You may have heard his voice on Focus on the Family, Moody Broadcasting, or Love Worth Finding. He has also written for Adventures in Odyssey and Radio Theatre.

Chris is a graduate of the W. Page Pitt School of Journalism at Marshall University in Huntington, West Virginia. He and his wife, Andrea, have been married 22 years and have nine children, two birds, two dogs, and one cat.

RED ROCK MYSTERIES

BRYCE AND ASHLEY TIMBERLINE are normal 13-year-old twins, except for one thing—they discover action-packed mystery wherever they go. Wanting to get to the bottom of any mystery, these twins find themselves on a nonstop search for truth.

CP0140

The Wormling

From the minds of Jerry B. Jenkins and Chris Fabry comes a thrilling new action-packed fantasy that pits ultimate evil against ultimate good.

Book I
The Book of the King

Book II
The Sword of the Wormling

Book III
The Changeling

Book IV
The Minions of Time

Book V
The Author's Blood

All 5 books available now!

CP0138